Tales of the Islanders

Tales of the Islanders

Charlotte Brontë

Hesperus Classics

Hesperus Classics
Published by Hesperus Press Limited
19 Bulstrode Street, London W1U 2JN
www.hesperuspress.com

First published 1925
First published by Hesperus Press Limited, 2011

Introduction © Jessica Cox, 2011

Designed and typeset by Fraser Muggeridge studio
Printed in Jordan by Jordan National Press

ISBN: 978-1-84391-201-9

CONTENTS

Introduction by Jessica Cox   vii

Tales of the Islanders   1
   Notes   83

Note on the text   *85*
Biographical note   *87*

INTRODUCTION

Charlotte Brontë's literary apprenticeship began many years before she published her first novel in 1847. During her childhood spent in Haworth parsonage in Yorkshire, Charlotte, along with her brother and sisters, Branwell, Emily and Anne, devoted much of her time to the world of her imagination, recording her creations in tiny, at times almost illegible handwriting. Some of these manuscripts were made into minuscule, handmade books – an effort that bears testament to the importance of these fictions to the Brontë children. The sheer volume of material which Charlotte produced in her teenage years alone is astounding, and the writing is suggestive of an irrepressible creative impulse. The earliest surviving writings by the Brontë children detail the origins of their stories, which developed from the gift of a set of toy soldiers presented to Branwell Brontë by his father Patrick. The four Brontë children each selected a soldier and created an identity for him, Charlotte choosing the Duke of Wellington – one of her childhood heroes and a figure who features repeatedly in her early writing. From this emerged the 'Young Men' plays, which in turn gave way to the 'Tales of the Islanders', also featuring Wellington, and later to the 'Glasstown' and 'Angria' stories. Out of the Brontë children's imaginations sprang sagas complete with vast kingdoms and characters exquisitely detailed. Brontë's juvenilia thus provides a fascinating insight into the developing mind of the writer who would eventually produce *Jane Eyre* – one of the most prevailingly popular novels in the English language.

Some of Charlotte Brontë's earliest surviving writing, 'Tales of the Islanders' was composed between July 1829 and July 1830, when incredibly, she was just thirteen years old. When

Elizabeth Gaskell, in the process of writing her biography of Charlotte Brontë, was given a packet containing some of Brontë's juvenile literary productions, she dismissed it as 'wild weird writing', and suggested that 'when she gives way to her powers of creation, her fancy and her language alike run riot, sometimes to the borders of apparent delirium.' However, although the writing is, as we might expect, in many respects immature, it nevertheless contains the germs of Charlotte Brontë's later literary productions, as well as providing an intriguing glimpse into the minds and experiences of the Brontë children.

Brontë's juvenilia is – as Elizabeth Gaskell implies – notable for its lack of restraint: years later, when she was trying to forge a career as a professional novelist, Charlotte was, inevitably, governed by her sense of the requirements of the literary marketplace, as well as by her desire to succeed not merely in terms of sales, but in terms of critical acclaim. No such influences govern her juvenile productions, however, which were intended for the eyes of the writer and her siblings only, and they are a heady mix of Gothic, sensational, grotesque and exotic elements, combined with social commentaries and insights into life at Haworth parsonage. 'Tales of the Islanders' serves as a representative example: historical events and personages are mingled with particulars of the Brontë children's daily lives, detailed descriptions of exotic lands, and accounts of fantastic adventures which include fairies, flying giants and sea monsters.

The 'Tales' begin with an account of their origins: Brontë describes how each of the four children, in December 1827, selected an island and a 'chief man' – Charlotte's again being the Duke of Wellington. The children themselves feature in the 'Tales' both by name and as the 'little King and Queens', manipulating events as both participants in and creators of this imaginary world. The volumes comprise a series of short, largely unconnected tales, which detail the adventures of the various characters. The 'Tales' as a whole are framed within Brontë's account of their creation, concluding with a further reference to the creators:

> *That is Emily's, Branwell's, Anne's and my land*
> *And now I bid a kind goodbye*
> *To those who o'er my book cast an indulgent eye.*

The individual stories also at times employ a frame narrative – a technique later employed by Emily and Anne Brontë in *Wuthering Heights* and *The Tenant of Wildfell Hall* respectively.

Many of the characters in the 'Tales' are based on public figures of the period – in particular, politicians of the day – a reflection of the young Brontë's interest in political and current affairs. Indeed, from an early age the Brontë children were encouraged by their father to take an interest in the world outside of the parsonage (a fact reflected in the social commentaries provided by their later novels): they had access to various newspapers, which the family would read and discuss together. The young Brontë children's somewhat surprising intense interest in politics, reflected in the choice of characters in 'Tales' as well as elsewhere in their juvenilia, is testament to the influence of this material. Charlotte's enthusiasm for political issues is apparent in her digressive discussion of the 'great Catholic question' at the beginning of Volume Two – an issue in which the Brontë family took a great interest: 'I remember the day when the *Intelligence Extraordinary* came with Mr Peel's speech in it containing the terms on which the

Catholics were to be let in; with what eagerness papa tore off the cover and how we all gathered round him and with what breathless anxiety we listened.' The issue of Catholicism is explored further in the 'Tales', offering a significant insight into the teenage Brontë's anti-Catholic prejudices, which she was to retain, to some degree, throughout her life. Chapter Five of Volume Two describes the conversion of an Irish man and his family from Catholicism to the Church of England, in spite of the evil machinations of a Catholic priest.

Though the 'Tales' clearly demonstrate the young Brontë's familiarity with and interest in current affairs, they also speak of an overwhelming concern with the fantastical. In this respect, they can be seen to engage with the Romantic tradition, by this time firmly established, and in particular with the fantastical creations of Samuel Taylor Coleridge, whose work, like the 'Tales', frequently combines elements of the Gothic, fantasy and the grotesque. Such features are particularly prominent in the final story of the 'Tales', in which an old man – a Muslim named Mirza Abduliemah – is transported to strange and exotic lands, encounters various weird and mystical creatures, including 'a vast army of giants', and is subject to an array of horrifying ordeals, culminating in his being burned to death in a sacrificial ceremony. The graphic description of his torture is suggestive of Brontë's burgeoning interest in the Gothic and the grotesque: 'he felt all the sinews crack the calcined bones started through his blackened cindery flesh.' The tale's blurring of the boundary between reality and dream again resonates with Romantic writings, such as Keats's 'Ode to a Nightingale': 'Was it a vision, or a waking dream? […] [D]o I wake or sleep?' Undoubtedly, the young Brontës' reading included the works of some of the most prominent figures of the Romantic movement –

Wordsworth, Byron and Southey – and these writers exerted a powerful influence on Charlotte Brontë's writing throughout her life. Indeed, as early Victorian novelists, the works of the Brontë sisters can be seen to straddle the boundary between Romanticism and Victorianism, and their early writing is clearly indebted to the literary productions of the Romantic poets.

At face value, the 'Tales' may appear to have little in common with Charlotte Brontë's later novels, but, although the writing is the product of an immature, still-developing mind, glimpses of the literary mind which would later emerge can nevertheless be seen. The authorial presence and the autobiographical elements of the narrative resonate with her later fiction, much of which was rooted in her own experiences. At times, the narrator of the 'Tales' intrudes on the narrative and addresses the reader directly, again anticipating a key aspect of her later work (as in the famous line which opens the final chapter of *Jane Eyre* – 'Reader, I married him'). The 'Tales' are also notable for their detailed descriptions of landscape and setting, and the weather in particular is frequently used symbolically, as in her later fiction. The reference to 'an oak [...] scathed by lightning' in the first volume of the 'Tales' seems to anticipate directly the destruction of the horse-chestnut tree in *Jane Eyre*. The blending of details of the Brontës' daily lives with elements of the Gothic, sensational and fantastical can also be seen to foreshadow Brontë's later fiction – in which realism is often combined uneasily with the dramatic and sensational. The 'Tales' include numerous references to strange portents and omens, and in this respect recall Jane Eyre's dreams and uncanny foreshadowing of the future, as well as the strange ghostly figure of the nun in *Villette*.

There are obvious and significant differences between Brontë's juvenilia and her later published work (not only in terms of literary merit, but also in terms of her early work's predominant focus on male experience, in contrast to her later concern with female experience). However, as a sample of Charlotte Brontë's early literary productions, 'Tales of the Islanders' forms part of a body of work that provides a valuable insight into her early life and influences, and her development as a writer.

– Jessica Cox, 2011

Tales of the Islanders

Volume 1

The *Play of the Islanders* was formed, in December 1827, in the following manner. One night, about the time when the cold sleet and dreary fogs of November are succeeded by the snow storms and high piercing nightwinds of confirmed winter, we were all sitting round the warm blazing kitchen fire, having just concluded a quarrel with Taby concerning the propriety of lighting a candle from which she came off victorious, no candle having been produced.[1] A long pause succeeded, which was at last broken by Branwell saying in a lazy manner, 'I don't know what to do.' This was re-echoed by Emily and Anne.

Taby: 'Wha' ya may go t'bed.'

Branwell: 'I'd rather do anything than that.'

Charlotte: 'You're so glum tonight. Well, suppose we had each an island.'

Branwell: 'If we had, I would choose the Island of Man.'

Charlotte: 'And I would choose the Isle of Wight.'

Emily: 'The Isle of Arran for me.'

Anne: 'And mine should be Guernsey.'

Charlotte: 'The Duke of Wellington should be my chief man.'[2]

Branwell: 'Herries should be mine.'

Emily: 'Walter Scott should be mine.'

Anne: 'I should have Bentinck.'[3]

Here our conversation was interrupted by the, to us, dismal sound of the clock striking seven and we were summoned off to bed. The next day we added several others to our list of names till we had got almost all the chief men in the kingdom.

After this, for a long time nothing worth noticing occurred. In June 1828, we erected a school on a fictitious island which was to contain a thousand children. The manner of the building was as follows: the island was fifty miles in circumference and certainly it appeared more like the region of enchantment or a beautiful fiction than sober reality. In some parts made terribly sublime by mighty rocks, rushing streams and roaring cataracts with here and there an oak either scathed by lightning or withered by time and, as if to remind the lonely passenger of what it once was, a green young scion twisting round its old grey trunk. In other parts of the island there were greenswards glittering, fountains springing in the flowery meadows or among the pleasant woods where fairies were said to dwell. Its borders embroidered by the purple, violet and the yellow primroses and the air perfumed by the sweet wild flowers and ringing with the sound of the cuckoo and turtledove or the merry music of the blackbird and thrush, formed the beautiful scenery.

One speciality around the palace school was a fine large park in which the beautiful undulations of hill and plain variegated the scenery which might otherwise have been monotonous. Shady groves crowned the hills, pure streams wandered through the plains watering the banks with a lovelier verdure, as clear lakes whose borders are overhung by the drooping willow, the elegant larch, the venerable oak and the evergreen laurel seemed the crystal, emerald-framed mirrors of some huge giant. Often at times it is said of one of the most beautiful of these lakes, that, when all is quiet, the music of fairyland may be heard and a tiny barge of red sandalwood, its mast of amber, its sails and cordage of silk and its oars of fine ivory may be seen skimming across the lake and, when its small crew have gathered the water lily plant, back again and, landing on the flowery bank, spread their transparent wings and melt away at the sound of mortal footsteps like the mists of the morning before the splendour of the sun.

From a beautiful grove of winter roses and twining wood-bine, towers a magnificent palace of pure white marble whose elegant and finely wrought pillars and majestic turrets seem the work of mighty Genii and not of feeble men. Ascending a flight of marble steps you come to a grand entrance which leads into a hall surrounded by Corinthian pillars of white marble. In the midst of the hall is a colossal statue holding, in each hand, a vase of crystal from which rushes a stream of clear water and, breaking into a thousand diamonds and pearls, falls into a basin of pure gold and, disappearing through an opening, rises again in different parts of the park in the form of brilliant fountains – these, falling, part into numerous rills which, winding through the ground, throw themselves into a river which runs into the sea.

At the upper end of the hall was a grove of orange trees bearing the golden fruit and fragrant blossoms, often upon the same branch. From this hall you pass into another splendid and spacious apartment, all hung with rich, deep, crimson velvet and from the grand dome is suspended a magnificent lustre of fine gold, the drops of which are pure crystal. The whole length of the room run long sofas covered also with crimson velvet. At each end are chimneypieces of dove-colour Italian marble, the pillars of which are of the Corinthian order, fluted and wreathed with gold. From this, we pass into a smaller but very elegant room, the sofas of which are covered with light-blue velvet flowered with silver and surrounded with small white marble columns.

And now from fine halls and splendid drawing rooms, I must begin to describe scenes of a very different nature. In the hall of the fountain, behind a statue, is a small door over which is drawn a curtain of white silk. This door, when opened, discovers a small apartment, at the further end of which is a very large iron door which leads to a long dark passage at the end of which is a flight of steps leading to a subterranean dungeon which I shall now endeavour to describe.

It has the appearance of a wide vault dimly lit by a lamp of asphalt which casts a strange death like lustre over part of the dungeon and leaves the rest in the gloom and darkness of midnight. In the middle is a slab of black marble supported by four pillars of the same. At the head of it stands a throne of iron. In several parts of the vault are instruments of torture for this place is the dreadful hall where wicked cockneys[4] are judged by that most unjust of judges: C.N. and his gang S, T.O.D and the rest.[5] At the end of this dungeon is the entrance to the cells which are appropriated to the private and particular use of Hal B. Stunt[6], the cockneys and the naughty schoolchildren. These cells are dark, vaulted, arched and so far down in the earth that the loudest shriek could not be heard by any inhabitant of the upper world, and in these, as well as the dungeon, the most unjust torturing might go on without any fear of detection if it was not that I keep the key of the dungeon and Emily keeps the key of the cells and the huge strong iron entrances will brave any assault except with the lawful instruments.

The children which inhabit this magnificent palace are composed only of the young nobles of the land, except such as Johnny Lockhart.[7] The chief governor under us is the Duke of Wellington. This, however, is only an honorary distinction as, when applied to, his Grace returned the following answer:

Little King and Queens (these are our titles),[8]
I am sorry to say my avocations of soldier and statesman will not allow me to comply with your requests that I would be governor of some hundreds, not to say any thousands, of

children, unless the title be merely honorary and I am to have
a few scores of subordinates under me.

With the request that it may be I remain your obedient
subject, W.

The request was complied with.

The guards for keeping the children in order and taking them out to walk are the Marquis of Douro[9] and Lord Charles Wellesley[10] for which they are peculiarly fitted as they lead them into the wildest and most dangerous parts of the country, leaping rocks, precipices, chasms etc. and little caring whether the children go before or stop behind and finally coming home with about a dozen wanting, who are found a few days after in hedges or ditches with legs or heads broken and affording a fine field for Sir A. Hume,[11] Sir A. Cooper[12] and Sir H. Halford[13] to display their different modes of setting and trepanning.

The guards for threshing the children when they do wrong (sometimes they exercise the privilege when they do not need it) are Colonel O'Shaugnesy and his nephew Fogharty. These are often eminently useful. I forgot to mention that Branwell has a large black club with which he thumps the children upon occasion and that most unmercifully. I have now done my notices of the school children for the present.

Among our islanders there are the Baines': three sons T., E. and T., who go by the separate names of Toltol, Nedned (or sometimes R.R. and Raten) and Tomtom.[14] These three are the most mischievous trio in existence: Tol is about two foot long, Nedned is half the length of his brother and Tom is three-quarters as long as Ned. Tol is dressed in a lawyer's gown and a huge wig which reaches to his feet and wraps round him; Rat is attired in a coarse piece of sackcloth tied round the neck and feet with rope and having the appearance of a tail and ears and Tom is dressed in the dress of a reporter.

About a year ago, as we were wandering in one of the woods which belong to the great domain of Strathfeildsay,[15] we heard a low voice behind us saying, 'There has been a storm today and the now blue and radiant arch of the mighty firmament has been overcast with dark clouds, the gloom of which was only broken by fierce gleams of lightning which shot across the black vapours like the word of revenge through the clouds; hatred which obscured the bright dawn of Whigish intellect! And I was appointed to be their avenger! Yes, this arm,' (here we saw an arm of little more than an inch long dart through the foliage), 'this arm shall wreak their spite upon the head of that stern Duke in whose domains I am. But soon I shall bring his pride down to the dust and make him bow. To the sovereign people.' Then with a rush through the tangled grass (for the spiteful creature did not reach higher than the grass) it reached the park gate, but here a great obstacle presented itself, for the keeper of the gate is an old veteran who has followed the Duke through all his wars and attended him in all his battles and if he had seen the animal he would certainly have taken it for a rat and would have treated it accordingly. Ned turned round and, seeing us, he said 'Little Queens will you open that gate?' As we wished to see the end of this adventure we took Raten up and threw him over the high wall and then knocked at the gate. We presently heard a rustling among the trees and the soldier stood before us.

Little Queen: 'If you please, Orderly-Man,[16] will you open that gate for us.'

Orderly-Man: 'I must first know who you are.'

Little Queen: 'We're little Queens.'

Orderly-Man: 'O, you are, are you? Come then.'

So saying, he opened the gate and we entered. Raten ran swiftly up the park and narrowly escaped been trodden to death by a deer which bounded close past him. There was, however, one thing which threatened to stop his progress and that was a river that gently and silently was winding its way through the park. For a while, he stood still on its banks and looked around, and behind him was the large wood he had just quitted. It was situated on a high hill and covered to the top with dark green foliage interspersed here and there with the lightly waving branches of the purple beech or the pale green of the white poplar. On each side of him lay the extensive and beautiful park, bounded by the wide domains of the great Duke, before him was the splendid mansion of Strathfeildsay and close to his feet was the river, on the opposite banks of which stood a deer – stooping its head and branching antlers to drink of the pure waters which flowed before it. On the branches of a young oak, which grew close by to the stream, sat a nightingale which was beginning its early song to the silver moon that now appeared like a pale crescent in the clear sky of the east. Over all the setting sun shed a golden radiance which invested everything with a splendour that made it appear like burning gold.

For a while, Raten seemed moved by the beauty of the scene but suddenly exclaiming 'R.R., no weakness!' he leaped into the river and, swimming across, he gained the opposite bank, then running with inconceivable swiftness up the rest of the park he reached the house, ran through the hall, the gallery, the stairs and at last reached the Duke's library. Nobody was there and upon the table stood a tumbler of water; into this Raten put something which however did not change its colour, then leaping from the table, he hid himself behind a large book which lay on the carpet.

Just then, the sound of footsteps was heard in the gallery, the door opened and a tall man with the air and carriage of a soldier entered, followed by another who was likewise tall but very stout. The first was his grace the Duke of Wellington and the second was Sir Alexander Hume. As soon as they entered, the Duke took from a shelf a volume and, sitting down, the following conversation ensued.

Wellington: 'Hume, what do you think of Walter Scott's *History of Napoleon*?'

Hume: 'Do you mean me to take the fact of it being written by a pekin[17] into consideration my lord?'

Wellington: 'Yes.'

Hume: 'Then, I think it is written as well as a pekin is capable of writing.'

Wellington: 'Do you think it has any truth in it?'

Hume: 'A great deal, my Lord.'

Wellington: 'You have given it a high meed of praise.'

Hume: 'Do you think I have praised it too highly?'

Wellington: 'Oh no.'

Hume: 'I would never wish to praise a pekin too much.'

After this a silence of about half an hour ensued and still the Duke did not touch the water. Raten began to be impatient and to fear for the success of his enterprise. At last his grace took up the glass and drained its contents. Raten was on the point of giving a shriek through joy but restrained himself. Just then Hume said, 'I never thought much good came of drinking cold water.' And a few minutes after, he exclaimed, 'My Lord are you well? How pale, how very pale you are. I never saw anybody more so.'

Here, Raten shouted out 'And pale he will always be.' The Duke fixed his stern eye on him and the creature shrank shuddering back to his corner. 'My Lord, are you dying? Ring the bell, little Queens.'

His Grace's features collapsed with agony, the volume fell from his hand and he sank back in his chair. Just then a loud yell rang in our ears, a rushing noise was heard and a giant of clouds stood before us. He touched the Duke and new life seemed to be given him. He stood up and in a firm tone demanded the name of the giant. It answered with a voice of thunder 'Mystery' and then slowly vanished.

His grace then ordered everyone out of his presence and a few days after Raten was found in his father's house at Leeds pale with horror trembling and half dead but how he got there is uncertain. Nor could he ever be induced to give any explanation and truly a mystery doth the whole affair remain to this day.

Prince Leopold[18] and Sir George Hill[19] have always entertained a great dislike to the Marquis of Douro and Lord Charles Wellesley. Prince Leopold, it is well known, is a very mean sort of personage with an appearance of cunning about him that is very disagreeable. Sir George Hill is frank and brave, somewhat given to gambling and an undue dislike of pekins. It has been lately surmised that he only pretends to dislike Arthur and Charles Wellesley for a little amusement and this is most likely true.

A little while ago, as Emily and me one stormy night were going through the wood which leads to school, we saw by the light of the moon which just then broke through a cloud, the flashing of some bright substance. The moon then became obscured and we could discern nothing more but see very black cloud. We heard a well-known voice saying, 'O, Arthur, I wish we had never come! What will my father say if he ever gets to know of it? And I am beginning to get very cold for it rains fast and the wind is high.'

'Wrap your fur cloak closer round you, Charles, and let us lean against this old tree for I shall not be able to stand much longer without some support. The sky is quite covered with dark clouds and how dismally the wind is moaning among the trees.'

'Arthur, what was that noise I heard? Listen.'

'It is a raven, Charles. I am not much given to superstition but I remember hearing my grandmother say it is a sign that something bad is coming to pass.'

'If we were to die here tonight and, remember, Arthur, we came here by appointment of two of our worst enemies, what would my mother do, and my father –'

Here they both sobbed aloud and we likewise heard a strange and horrible noise sweep through the wood.

'What is the matter with our dogs, Arthur? Are they dying?'

'No, Charles, but that likewise is said to be a sound of death.'

'A sound of death, Arthur! But listen again to the raven. O! this is a dreadful place.'

'Hush, Charles! They are coming.'

The glimmering of a lantern appeared through the trees and two men burst upon the path. One of them was tall and bony but he had an expression of pity in his face as he said, 'Poor fellows! Though I don't particularly like you, yet I'm sorry you've had to wait so long in the rain this cold night –'

The other was a mean despicable wretch and he squinted.

'Prince Leopold and Sir George Hill, we are quite ready to follow you but go slowly for we cannot possibly walk fast.'

'Come along then.'

So saying, they set off and we followed close behind. By the light of the lantern we could see that the Marquis of Douro and Lord Charles Wellesley had two bloodhounds with them

14

and as soon as they emerged from the forest these two dogs gave a dreadful yell. Prince Leopold shook with terror and Charles patted them at which they moaned piteously. After this they were silent for a while and the march proceeded. After climbing a great many high steep rocks and leaping many ditches we entered on the confines of the great moor. Just then the bloodhounds stopped again and gave another horrible cry which rang all over the wide heath and seemed to be answered from a great distance with a deeper and more dreadful yell.

'Do make your nasty dogs hold their tongues or else I will,' said Sir George.

'If you touch them, Hill, you must take the consequences,' answered Arthur, 'they might bite you.'

Leopold was panting with fear.

'Come on boys,' shouted Sir George with a peal of hollow laughter which was answered by the echoing rocks with ten-fold vehemence. Just at that moment a dull flapping of wings and an ominous croak was heard.

'What in the name of wonder is that?'

'It's a raven!' replied Leopold almost fainting with cowardice.

'Oh! Do make haste that we may reach some shelter for the darkness of the night is increasing, the rain is falling faster and the wind sweeps with more fearful blast over this wild bleak moor.'

They all moved on and after a while a light became visible on the verge of the horizon which as they approached it, vanished, but by the help of the lantern we could discern a small and seemingly deserted cottage. They entered it and we followed by a door which was decayed by time and shattered by violence in many places.

'And is this where you intend to take us?' exclaimed the Marquis of Douro.

'Oh no, but as you seem unable to go any further, I thought you had better stop here and very likely we shall find some of our friends below,' said Sir George as he opened a door which discovered a narrow flight of steps down which they went. And then came to another door and now likewise they heard a sound of many voices and much mirth. Sir George opened the door and immediately a blaze of light and genial warmth burst forth which almost overpowered them after being so long exposed to the dark wet night. The cellar into which they came was vaulted and the lime dropping off the wall in many parts. There was a large peat fire blazing on the hearth and on benches round sat a great many officers among whom was the Marquis of A., Lords C.A.W. and G.P.[20] Some were drinking, some playing at cards, singing and yet as soon as the Marquis of Douro and Lord Charles Wellesley saw these things they exclaimed:

'We will go no further and, though we die for it, we had rather stop all night on the open moor than in this wicked place and if you prevent us from going hence it will be at your peril.'

'Will it?' said Leopold with a shrill, scornful laugh.

They called their dogs which however did not make their appearance. Leopold then rushed towards them, threw them down and gagged them and tied their hands and feet then returning to the party round the fire he began to play sing and be as loud and talkative as any among them. But in the midst of all this mirth and cheerfulness the sound of footsteps was heard descending the stairs the door was burst open and two men followed by three large dogs burst into the apartment. One of the men was instantly known by his stern countenance and flashing eye as he exclaimed with fierce energy, 'You wretches, where are my sons?' It was the Duke of Wellington. They were too much astounded to reply till he repeated the question more fiercely than before and commanded them to give him an answer. Leopold replied tremblingly, 'They are there.'

'They are! You vile beggar!' said his Grace and kicked him to the opposite end of the cellar then, going to the corner which Leopold had pointed to, he unbound and ungagged his sons and raised them up. They were, however, unable to stand and fell back again. His Grace then turned to the rest and said in a tone of voice which showed he meant to be obeyed, 'I command you all to quit this place and if ever you return here again I shall make you suffer for it and that dreadfully.'

Immediately, they flung open the door rushed up the stair and scampered off as fast as they could. In the meantime, the other man, who was Doctor Hume, had given Arthur and Charles something which strengthened them so much that they could stand and even walk. The Duke then inquired how they came to that house. Just at this moment we issued from our hiding place and related all the circumstances after which we asked how his Grace got to know of Charles and Arthur being there. His Grace told us that as he was on his way to school, accompanied by Hume and his great bloodhound, he thought he heard at a distance the yelling of his sons' dogs which was immediately answered by his own and that, after he had gone about a mile further he met a countryman who told him that he had seen his sons on the great moor in the company of George Hill and Prince Leopold that then, though it was night, he rode towards the moor but was met on his way by his sons' dogs who led them to the cottage.

As soon as his Grace had finished he rose to depart and Arthur and Charles followed. When they had got up the dark narrow stairs and to the door of the cottage they were surprised to find the rising sun beaming through the chinks of the door and, when they reached the open air, the scenes which greeted their eyes were truly refreshing. Instead of dark watery clouds, there was the blue radiant dome-like sky in which the pale moon was yet visible. The glorious sun was rising in the east and making the rain which had fallen the preceding night, and which still remained on the balmy heath, sparkle like fine diamonds. A few little wild mountain sheep were to be seen and as they drew near they scurried away and sprang up the rocks till they could view us safely at a distance. The lark sprang from his mossy bed at our approach and began to warble its matin song and the higher it mounted up in the blue heavens the sweeter did its song become till it could no longer be heard. In a short time they came to the edge of the moor and reached school about nine o'clock all sound in life and limb. Thus ended the Duke's, Marquis' and Lord's adventure of the cottage.

Volume 2

CHAPTER 1

I have before put forth a volume of these tales in which the subject of the school was mentioned, in that volume I laid down the rules by which the school was governed and likewise the names of the governors with their several characters etc. I shall now proceed with this subject.

For some time after it was established, the institution went on very well. All the rules were observed with scrupulous exactness, the governors attended admirably to their duty, the children were absolutely becoming something like civilised beings, to all outward appearance at least, gambling was less frequent among them, their quarrels with each other were less savage and some little attention was paid by themselves to order and cleanliness. At this time we constantly resided in the magnificent palace of the school as did all the governors so that nothing was left entirely to the care of servants and underlings. The great room had become the resort of all the great ministers in their hours of leisure (that is in the evenings) and they, seeing how well were conducted, resolved to uphold the institution with all their might.

This prosperous state of affairs continued for about six months and then parliament was opened and the great Catholic question was brought forward and the Duke's measures were disclosed and all was slander, violence, party spirit and confusion. O, those three months, from the time of the King's speech to the end! Nobody could think, speak or write on anything but the Catholic question and the Duke of Wellington or Mr Peel. I remember the day when the *Intelligence Extraordinary* came with Mr Peel's speech in it containing the terms on which the Catholics were to be let in; with what eagerness papa tore off the cover and how we all gathered round him and with what breathless anxiety we listened as, one by one, they were disclosed and explained and argued upon so ably and so well.[21] And then, when it was all out, how Aunt said she thought it was excellent and that the Catholics could do no harm with such good security. I remember also the doubts as to whether it would pass into the House of Lords and the prophecies that it would not. When the paper came which was to decide the question the anxiety was almost dreadful with which we listened to the whole affair – the opening of the doors, the hush, the royal dukes in their robes and the great Duke in green sash and waistcoat, the rising of all the peeresses when he rose, the reading of his speech, Papa saying that his words were like precious gold and, lastly, the majority one to four in favour of the Bill. But this is a digression and I must beg my readers to excuse it – to proceed with my subject then.

In consequence of this Catholic question, the Duke and Mr Peel were, of course, obliged to be constantly in London and we soon took ourselves off to the same place. O'Shaugnesy and his nephew were away shooting somewhere and the whole management of the school was left to the Marquis of Douro and Lord Charles Wellesley. The upshot will be seen in the next chapter.

CHAPTER 2

For some time we heard not a word about the school and never took the trouble to inquire until, at length, one morning, as we were sitting at breakfast, in came a letter the which, when we had opened, we perceived was from my Lord Wellesley. The purport was as follows:

June 8, Vision Island

Little King and Queens
I write this letter to inform you of a rebellion which has broken out in the school, the particulars of which I have not time to relate: all I can say is that I am at present in a little hut built in the open air – and – but they are coming and I can say no more –

I remain yours etc –

Charles W

P.S. Since I wrote the above, we have had a battle in which our bloodhounds fought bravely and we have conquered – we are however reduced to a great extremity for want of food and if you don't make haste and come to our help we must surrender. Bring my father's great bloodhound with you and Doctor Hume and the Gamekeeper[22] likewise –

As soon as we had read this letter, we ordered a balloon the which, when it was brought, we got into and then steered our way through the air towards Strathfeildsay. When we had there arrived, we took up bloodhounds and the Gamekeeper and then went quick-way to the island. We alighted in the grounds about the school and, on casting our eyes towards the myrtle grove, we saw the stately palace rising in its magnificence from the green trees which grew thickly around and towering in silent grandeur over that isle which was rightly named a dream, for never but in the visions of the night has the eye of man beheld such gorgeous beauty, such wild magnificence as is in this fairy land and never but in the imaginings of his heart has his ear heard such music as that which proceeds from the giant's harp, hid from sight amid those trees. Listen, there is a faint sound like the voice of a dying swan but now a stronger breeze sweeps through the strings and the music is rising. Hark how it swells! What grandeur was in that wild note, but the wind roars louder. I heard the muttering of distant thunder, it is drawing nearer and nearer and the tunes of the harp and swelling till, all at once, amidst the roaring of thunder and the howling of the wind it peals out with such awful wildness, such unearthly grandeur that you are tempted to believe it is the voice of spirits speaking. This is the storm.

But to proceed with my subject: after we had been in the island about half an hour we saw Lord Wellesley approaching at a distance. When he came near, he accosted us with, 'Well, little Queens, I am glad you are come. Make haste and follow me for there is not a moment to be lost.' As we went along, he, at our request, gave us the following narrative as to the origin of the school rebellion.

'For about three days after you were gone things went on very well but, at the end of that time, symptoms of insubordination began to manifest themselves. These we strove to check but in vain and instead of growing better they grew worse. The school now was divided into four parties each of which was headed by a chieftain namely Prince Polignac,[23] Prince George,[24] Johny Lockhart and the Princess Vittoria.[25] These four were constantly quarrelling and fighting with each other, in a most outrageous manner and, after struggling a few weeks with them, to no purpose, they all ran off and are now encamped in a very wild part of the island which we shall presently come to. They are well provided with two cannons to each party and a quantity of powder and shot. Sometimes they all unite against us and then we have a bad chance, I assure you, but now you are come to our assistance we shall soon do for them.'

As soon as he had ended, we emerged from the forest in which we had till then been travelling and entered a deep glen through which rushed an impetuous, brawling river roaring and foaming amongst the large stones which impeded its course and then, as its channel deepened and widened, it became calm and smooth flowing silently through the wide green plain on the right hand, fertilising and refreshing it as it went. On our left arose rocks frowning darkly over the glen and blackening it with their mighty shadow. In some parts, they were covered with tall pine trees through which the wind moaned sadly as it swept among their scathed branches. In other parts, immense fragments of rock looked out from their shaggy covering and hung their grey summits awfully over the vale. No sound but the echo of a distant cannon which was discharged as we entered the glen and the scream of the eagle startled from her eyrie disturbed the death-like silence.

In a short time, we came to the place where the children were encamped. The tents of the Vitorans were pitched on the summit of a rock, those of the Polignacs in a deep ravine, the Georgians had taken up their abode in an open spot of ground and the Lockhartians had entrenched themselves among some trees. The hut of the Marquis of Douro and Lord Wellesley was built beneath the shade of a spreading oak. A tremendous rock rose above it. On one side was a gently swelling hill, on the other a grove of tall trees and before it ran a clear rippling stream.

When we had entered the humble abode, we beheld the Marquis of Douro lying on a bed of leaves. His face was very pale; his fine features seemed as fixed as a marble statue. His eyes were closed and his glossy curling hair was, in some parts, stiffened with blood. As soon as we beheld this sight, Charles rushed forward and, falling on the bed beside his brother, he fainted away. The usual remedies were then applied to him by Doctor Hume and, after a long time, he recovered. All this while, Arthur had neither spoken nor stirred and we thought he was dead. The Gamekeeper was raving and even the hardhearted Hume shed some tears and Charles seemed like one demented. In this emergency we thought it advisable to send quick-way for the Duke of Wellington. This we accordingly did and as soon as we saw him coming one of us went out to meet him. When we had informed him of what had happened he became as pale as death; his lips quivered and his whole frame shook with agitation. In a short time, he arrived at the hut and then, going up to the bedside, he took hold of one lifeless hand and said in a tremulous and scarcely audible voice, 'Arthur, my son, speak to me.' Just then at the sound of his father's words, Arthur slowly opened his eyes and looked up. When he saw the Duke, he tried to speak but could not. We then, in the plenitude of our goodness and kindness of heart, cured him instantaneously by the application of some fairy remedies and, as soon as we had done so, the Duke drew from his finger a diamond ring and presented it to us. This we accepted and thanked him for it.

After these transactions we informed his Grace of the school rebellion. He immediately went out without speaking a word and we followed him. He proceeded up to the place were they were encamped and called out, in a loud tone of voice, that if they did not surrender they were all dead men as he had brought several thousand bloodhounds with him who would tear them to pieces in a moment. This they dreaded more than anything and therefore agreed to surrender which they did immediately and for a short time thereafter the school prospered as before but we, becoming tired of it, sent the children off to their own homes and now only fairies dwell in the island of a dream.

CHAPTER 3

About a year after the school rebellion, the following wonderful thing happened in the family of the Duke of Wellington. One pleasant morning in the month of September 1828, the Marquis of Douro and Lord Charles Wellesley went out to follow the sport of shooting. They had promised to return before eight o'clock but however ten o'clock came and they had not returned: twelve and still no signs of them. Old Man Cockney[26] then ordered the servants to bed and, when they had retired and all was quietness, he went into the great hall and sat down by the fire, determined not to go to bed till they came back. He had sat about half an hour listening anxiously for their arrival when the inner door gently opened and Lady Wellesley appeared. Old Man could see by the light of the fire, for he had put out the candle, that she was very pale and much agitated.

'What is the matter, madam?' said he.

Lady Wellesley: 'I was sitting down working when suddenly I saw the light cast on my work by the taper turn blue and death like burning phosphorous or asphaltas. I looked up and saw the figures of my sons all bloody and distorted. I gazed on them till they vanished unable to speak or stir and then I came down here.'

She had scarcely finished the recital of this strange vision when the great door was heard to open with a loud, creaking noise and the Duke of Wellington entered. He stood still for a moment earnestly looking at Lady Wellesley and the Old Man and then said in a distinctly audible but hollow tone of voice, 'Catherine, where are my sons, for I heard, while sitting in my study, their voices moaning and wailing around me and supplicating me to deliver them from the death they were about to die, even now I feel a dreadful foreboding concerning them which I cannot shake off. Catherine, where are they?'

Before Lady Wellesley could answer, the door again opened and we appeared. He immediately addressed us and begged of us to tell him what had become of them. We replied that we did not know but that if he liked we would go in search of them. He thanked us gratefully, adding that he would go with us, and then after he had taken leave of Lady Wellesley we immediately set off.

We had gone as near as we could, about four miles, when we entered a very wild barren plain which none of us had ever seen before. We continued on this plain till we lost sight of everything else and then suddenly perceived the whole aspect of the sky to be changed. It assumed the appearance of large rolling waves, crested with white foam, also we could hear a thundering sound, like the roaring of the sea at a distance, and the moon seemed a great globe of many miles in diameter. We were gazing in silent astonishment at this glorious sight, which every minute was growing grander and grander, and the noise of thunder was increasing when suddenly the huge waves parted asunder and a giant, clothed in the sun with a crown of twelve stars on his head, descended on the plain. For a moment our sight was destroyed by the glory of his apparel and, when it was restored to us, we found ourselves in a world the beauty of which exceeds beyond my powers of description. There were trees and bowers of light, waters of liquid crystal flowing over sands of gold with a sound the melody of which far exceeds music of the finest-toned harps or the song of the sweet-voiced nightingales. There were palaces of emerald, of ruby, of diamond, of amethyst and pearl arches like the rainbow of jasper agate and sapphire spanning wide seas whose mighty voices were now hushed into a gentle murmur and sang in sweet unison with the silver streams which flowed through this radiant land, while their glorious song was echoed and re-echoed by high mountains which rose in the distance and which shone in the glowing light like fine opals set in gold.

We had been here for a short time when the sky blackened, the winds rose, the waves of the ocean began to roar. All beautiful things vanished and were succeeded by tall dark cypress and fir trees which swayed to and fro in the wind with a mournful sound, like the moans of dying mortals. A huge black rock appeared before us and a wide and dark cavern opened in it, in which we saw Arthur and Charles Wellesley. The giant then came again and taking them and us in his arms flew swiftly through the air and landed us all in the great hall of Strathfeildsay.

CHAPTER 4

It was a beautiful evening in the month of August when the Duke of Wellington and his sons were seated in a small private parlour at the top of the great round tower at Strathfeildsay. The sun was just setting and its beams shone through the gothic window, half-veiled by a green velvet curtain which had fallen from the golden supports and hung in rich festoons, with a glowing brilliance equal to the crimson light which streams from the oriental ruby but, unlike to that beautiful gem, it was every moment decreasing in splendour till, at length, only a faint rose tint remained on the marble pedestal which stood opposite bearing the statue of William Pitt and which, but a little while ago, had shone with a brightness resembling the lustre of burnished gold. Just as the last ray disappeared, Lord Charles Wellesley exclaimed, 'Father, I wish you would relate to us some of your adventures either in India or Spain.'

'Very well, I will, Charles. Now listen attentively,' replied his Grace, 'would you like to hear too, Arthur?'

'I should very much,' answered the Marquis with a gravity and calmness which formed a striking contrast to the giddy gaiety that marred the deportment of his younger brother.

His Grace began as follows: 'In the year and the day of the battle of Salamanca, just as the sun set and the twilight was approaching, I finished my despatches and walked forth from the convent gates of the Rector of Salamanca in order to enjoy the coolness of a Spanish evening. To this purpose, I proceeded through the city till I came to the outside of its walls and then strolled heedlessly along by the clear stream of the Tormes, following as it led until I found myself far away from the city and on the borders of a great wood which stretched over many high hills to the verge of the horizon: there was a small pathway cut through this forest, which I entered, striding over the river which had now dwindled into a diminutive rill. Strictly speaking this was not a prudent step nor one which I should advise you, my sons, if ever you should be in the like circumstances to take, for the evening was far advanced and the bright light of the beautiful horizon cast an uncertain glowing glare on everything which made travelling through a dark wood which I knew nothing of exceeding dangerous, the country was likewise much infested with daring robbers and organised banditti who dwelt in such lonely situations, but there was a sort of charm upon me which led me on in spite of myself. After I had proceeded about a quarter of a mile, I heard a sound like music at a distance which in a short time died away, but when I had got very deep into the forest it rose again and then it sounded nearer, I sat down under a large spreading maple tree whose massive limbs and foliage were now beginning to be irradiated by the moonlight which pierced into the depths of the forest and highly illumined with its beams the thick darkness. I had not sat here long when suddenly the music which had till then sounded soft and low like the preluding of a fine musician on a sweet instrument, broke out into a loud deep strain which resembled the pealing of a full toned organ when its rich floods of sound are rolling and swelling in the sublime *Te Deum* and echoing amid the lofty aisles and high dome of some grand cathedral with a deep solemn noise like the loud awful rumbling and terrible thunder, or the sudden burst of that most sublime of all music martial music when the ringing trumpet and the rolling drum are sounding together with the fierce onset of a brave and noble army. Then you feel the grandeur of the battle, amid the lightning and roar of the cannon, the glancing of swords and lances and the thunder of the living cataract of men and horses rushing terribly to victory, who stands arrayed in bloody garments with a crown of glory upon her head. But to proceed with my story, no sooner had this loud concert sounded than the dark forest vanished, like mists of the morning before the sun's brightness, and slowly there rose up on my sight a huge mirror, in which were dimly shadowed the forms of clouds and vapours, all dense and black, rolling one over the other in dark and stormy grandeur and among them, in letters of lightning I saw the "Futurity". By degrees these clouds cleared away and a fair and beautiful island appeared in their stead rising out of the midst of a calm and peaceful ocean and linked to it by a golden chain was another equal in beauty but smaller. In the middle of the largest of these two islands was a tall and majestic female seated on a throne of ruby, crowned with roses, bearing, in one hand, a wreath of oak leaves and in the other a sword, while, over her, the tree of liberty flourished, spreading its branches far and wide and casting the perfume of its flowers to the uttermost parts of the earth. In the midst of the other island there was likewise a female who sat on an emerald throne. Her crown was formed of shamrocks, in her right hand she held a harp and her robes were of a crimson hue as if they had been dyed in blood. She was as majestic as the other but in her countenance was something very sad and sorrowful, as if a terrible evil hung upon her – over her head were the boughs of a dark cypress instead of the pleasant tree which shaded the other island, and sometimes she swept the chords of the harp causing a wild and mournful sound to issue therefrom like a death wail or dirge. While I was wondering at her grief, I perceived a tremendous monster rise out of the sea and land on her island. As soon as it touched the shores, a lamentable cry burst forth which shook both islands to their centre and the ocean all round boiled furiously as if some terrible earthquake had happened. The monster was black and hideous and the sound of his roaring was like thunder. He was clothed in the skin of wild beasts and in his forehead was branded as with a hot iron the word "Bigotry". In one hand, he held a scythe and, as soon as he entered the land, the work of desolation began: all pleasantness and beauty disappeared from the face of the country and pestilential morasses came in their stead. He seemed to pursue with inveterate fury a horrible old man who, a voice whispered in my ear, was called the Romish Religion. At first he seemed weak and impotent but, as he ran, he gathered strength and the more he was persecuted, the stronger he became till, at length, he began with a terrible voice to defy his persecutor and at the same time strove to break the golden chain which united the two islands. And now I saw the form of a warrior approaching whose likeness I could by no means discern but over whom a mighty shield was extended from the sky. He came near to the monster whose name was bigotry and, taking a dart on which the word "Justice" was written in golden characters, he flung it at him with all his might. The dart had struck in the heart and he fell with a loud groan to the earth. As soon as he had fallen, the warrior whose brow had already many wreaths on it was crowned by a hand which proceeded from a golden cloud with a fresh one of amaranths interwoven with laurel. At the same time, the two spirits arose from their thrones and, coming towards him, they cast garlands and crowns of victory at his feet while they sung his praises in loud and glorious notes. Meantime, the desolated land was again overspread with pleasant pastures and green woods and sunny plains watered by clear rivers flowing with a gentle sound over green rocks, while the wild harp pealed in sweetly swelling tones among the branches of the tree of liberty. The sound ceased and, lo, I was beneath the maple tree and a nightingale was serenading me with its beautiful song which caused me to dream of sweet music.'

CHAPTER 5

In the year 1722, in the pleasant month of June, four inhabitants of fairyland took it into their heads, for a treat, to pay a visit to the inhabitants of the earth. In order to accomplish this end, they took the form of mortals, but first it was necessary to obtain leave of Oberon and Titania, their King and Queen. Accordingly they demanded an audience of their majesties and were admitted. They stated their wish and petition which was immediately granted and they prepared to depart.

Having descended to the earth in a cloud, they alighted in a part of England which was very mountainous and quite uninhabited. They proceeded along for some time till they came to the verge of a rock that looked down into a beautiful vale below. Through it ran a clear and pleasant stream which followed the vale in all its narrow windings among the high dark mountains which bordered it and the massive branching trees which grew in thick clumps casting a cool and agreeable shade over all the valley. Through these, it meandered with a rippling sound until when the glen broke from its confinement among them and spread into a wide green plain all dotted with great white poplars and stately oaks and spangled with pearly daisies and golden buttercups among which likewise occasionally peeped out the pale primrose or the purple violet. It also expanded into a broader and deeper current rolling, or rather gliding, on with a still murmur that resembled the voice of some water spirit heard from the depths of its coral palaces when it sings in lonely silence after the sea has ceased to heave and toss in terrible black beauty and night walks in awful majesty on the face of the earth all clothed in stars while Luna sheds pale light from her silver lamp to illumine the pathway of the dark and stately queen. In the midst of this valley, there was a small thatched cottage which had once been the pleasant abode of a flourishing husbandman who was now dead and his children had, one by one, forsaken it and the sweet spot where it stood, each to pursue his own fortune till it was now entirely deserted and had fallen into a state of ruin and decay.

The fairies proceeded down the vale towards the cottage and when they arrived there began to examine it. The walls were all grey and moss grown; vine tendrils were still visible among the wreaths of ivy which clasped around the doorway and one silver star of a jesamine peeped out from among the dark leaves. The little garden was all grown over with nettles and rank weed and no trace remained of its former beauty except a single rose bush on which still bloomed a few half-wild roses and beside it grew a small strawberry plant with two or three scarlet strawberries upon it forming a fine contrast to the desolation which surrounded them.

In this place the fairies determined to take up their abode, which they accordingly did and they had not been long their when the following occurrence happened. They were sitting one evening round the fire of their hut (for being now in the form of mortals they acted like them) listening to the wind which moaned in hollow cadences as it swept along the valley and its voice was sometimes mingled with strange sounds which they well knew were the voices of spirits rising in the air, invisible to the dull eyes of mortals. They were sitting, as I said before, around the fire of their hut when suddenly they heard a low knocking at the door. One of them immediately rose to open it and a man appeared clothed in a traveller's cloak. They enquired what he wanted. He replied that he had lost his way in the glen and that seeing the light stream across his path from their cottage he had stopped there and now requested shelter till the morning when he might be able to pursue his journey with the advantage of daylight. His request was immediately granted and, as soon as he was seated, they asked what the cause of his travelling was. He replied that, if they chose, he would relate to them his whole history as he could perceive that they were persons of no ordinary description and might perhaps be able to assist him in his distress. They consented and he began as follows:

'I am the son of a gentleman of great fortune and estate who resided in one of the southernmost counties of Ireland. My father and mother were both Roman Catholics and I was brought up in that faith and continued in it until I became convinced of the error of the creed I professed. My father's confessor was a man of strange and unsociable habits and was thought by those among whom he dwelt to have converse with the inhabitants of another world. He had received his education in Spain and it was supposed that in the country he had learnt the science of necromancy. The manner in which I became converted to the Protestant religion was as follows. There lived in our family an old servant who unknown to my father was a seceder from the Roman Catholic Church and a member of the Church of England. One day I unexpectedly entered the room and surprised him reading his Bible. I immediately remonstrated with him on the impropriety of what he was about and desired him to leave off, telling him that it was against the laws of the true church and contrary to the admonitions of our priest. He replied mildly but firmly quoting many passages of scripture in defence of what he did and arguing in such a manner as to convince me that I was in the wrong. Next day, I paid him a visit at the same hour and found him similarly employed. I had a long conversation with him, the effect of which was to induce me to search the Bible for myself: I did so and there discovered that the doctrines of the Church of England where those which most closely assimilated with the word of God, those doctrines I accordingly determined to embrace. As soon as my conversion became known, my father strove to dissuade me from it, but I remained steadfast and resolute. In a short time he ceased to trouble me. But not so with the confessor: he was constantly advancing arguments to induce me to recant but, failing, he made use of the following expedient, as a last resource. I was standing one evening in the court of my father's house, when suddenly I heard a voice whisper in my ear, "Come this night to the great moor at twelve o'clock." I turned round but could see nobody. I then debated with myself what it could be and whether I should go or not. I, at length, determined to go and when the clock struck eleven I set off. The moor alluded to lay about four miles off, it was a wide barren heath stretching three leagues to the northward. In a short time, I reached it. The night was very dark, no moon was visible and the stars were only dimly seen through the thin cloudy vapours that sailed over the sky, veiling the dark azure with a sombre robe and casting a melancholy gloom on the path beneath. All around me was silent except a little stream, flowing unseen among the heather with a sound resembling the hoarse incessant murmur which the seashell retains of its native caverns where the green billows of the deep are roaring and raging with an eternal thunder. I had not waited long when, slowly, I saw rising around me the dim form of a sacred abbey, the stately pillars, the long drawn sweeping aisles, the echoing dome and the holy altar all arose in gradual and mysterious order while a solemn and supernatural light stole through the high-arched windows and beamed full upon a tomb which stood in the centre and which I knew to be my grandfather's. I was gazing at these things in rapt and silent astonishment, when suddenly I saw a tall, white-robed figure standing upon the monument. It beckoned to me with its hand: I approached and it then addressed me in the following words, "Son, why have you deserted the ancient and holy religion of your ancestors to embrace a strange one which you know not of?"

I was going to reply when, at that moment, I perceived the confessor standing near. I instantly comprehended the whole scheme and exclaimed in a loud voice, "Your wiles are discovered. The faith I profess is true and I well know that this is all necromancy." When the priest heard this, he flew into a terrible rage and, stamping with his foot, a fire sprung out of the ground. He then threw some perfumes on it and said, in a voice made tremulous by ungovernable fury, "Depart hence vile heretic!" and immediately I found myself in this valley. You know the rest.'

Here the traveller stopped and little more is known of the story except that the fairies restored him to his family who became devout members of the Church of England. The priest afterwards disappeared in a very unaccountable way and the fairies no longer dwell in that little hut of which only a mossy remnant now remains but the tradition still lives in many a peasant's fireside tale when gloomy winter has apparelled the earth in frost and radiant snow.

This tale was related to little King and Queens, Seringapatan,[27] Old Man Cockney, Gamekeeper, Jack of all Trades[28] and Orderly-Man by the Marquis of Douro and Lord C. Wellesley as they sat by the fire at the great hall of Strathfeildsay.

Volume 3

CHAPTER 1

One evening, the Duke of Wellington was writing in his room at Downing Street. Eldon[29] reposed at his ease in an ample easy chair, smoking a homely tobacco pipe (for he disdained all the modern frippery of cigars etc), beside a blazing fire whose flames Left had just been feeding by a fresh supply of Londonderry's black diamonds. One-armed Hardinge stood at his desk awkwardly scrawling an army estimate on a gilt-edged sheet of Bath post.[30] Coxcombical Roslyn[31] lounged against the polished green marble mantelpiece, eyeing with ineffable contempt the quizzical old pekin, who sat opposite and occasionally casting a sidelong glance at his own dandy figure reflected in a magnificent mirror, suspended against the wall which was hung with purple figured velvet; Castlereagh,[32] seated on a Turkish Ottoman, whined and yawned incessantly while Mr Secretary Peel[33] perched upon a treasury tripod close beside his Grace kept whispering and wheedling in the Duke's ear until, at length, happening to interrupt him in the midst of an abstruse calculation, he saw his master's eye suddenly flash on him and without further warning was at the other end of the room in a twinkling. At this tragic catastrophe, Roslyn slunk back to his desk which he had quitted without leave from headquarters. Hardinge just gave a keck over his shoulder at the prostrate civilian. Eldon ceased puffing, holding up his withered hands half in fear and half in wonder; Castlereagh crawled off the cushion under the table where he lay quietly down and the Duke of Wellington, without noticing the general consternation, relapsed into his former occupation of unravelling a confused mass of exchequer-like figures left by poor Vesey in a sad state of disorder when he was seized with the sickness which superannuated him.

While they were thus employed, a heavy footstep was heard without. The door opened and a little shrunken old woman wrapped up and wholly concealed except her face entered. Her appearance excited no surprise for this was one of the famous little Queens. She advanced up to the Duke and presented him a letter written with blood and sealed with a seal on which was the motto '*le message d'un revenant*'. He took it respectfully and read it, while he was doing this, he changed colour several times evincing an uncontrollable emotion. When he had finished he rose and walked about as if trying to calm his mind. Suddenly, he stopped and commanded all present to depart: they immediately obeyed. Then, after a pause, he demanded of the fairy if that letter was true or a forgery. She made a sign with her hand and immediately the king and the two other Queens appeared. They all knelt down. Each drew out a wand wreathed with ivory; they kissed them and said, 'It is by virtue of these wands we rule the hearts of mortals. We will forfeit them and our spiritual power if what we say is false. That letter is true.' When they had uttered these words, they vanished.

His Grace immediately rang a bell and ordered the attendant who answered the summons to get ready the swiftest horse in his stables. His mandates were presently obeyed and the Duke clad in a Georgian mantle with a broad military belt, brass helmet and high black plumes, mounted the spirited animal, spurred him to full gallop and in a short time left London and its suburbs far behind. He rode with such speed that, when the sun rose, he beheld the towers of Strathfeildsay rearing their proud heads, ruddy with the first beams of morning from the ancient oak forests which surrounded them. All his wide domains were stretched before his eyes, the peaceful village nestling among venerable woods, the wide fruitful fields extending to the verge of the horizon, the stately trees darkening the scene with their shadow, the white cottages looking out from the bowery retreat of their orchard and the great river refreshing everything as it passed. All were his own, won by his invincible sword, the monuments of England's gratitude to her glorious preserver.

He passed quickly on and in a short time arrived at the dark gate. The old soldiers' cottages removed a little way from the narrow path could hardly be distinguished by reason of the large trees on each side whose thick drooping branches now in full verdure had shot out and increased to such a degree as wholly to surround them with a fresh verdant barrier and their situation was only marked by the tall, round grey chimneys, one of which (that on the right hand) belonging to Seringapatan was just breathing a light dun smoke on the stainless ether. The other stood in motionless silence for the inhabitants thereof, to wit Jack of all Trades, Orderly-Man and Gamekeeper, were for the present tarrying at the more noisy and, to their dispositions, (unlike that of their bookish neighbour) more congenial Horse Guards.

His Grace was just in the act of raising a huge bough which guarded the right-hand doorway, for the purpose of entering, when he heard a light buoyant step and a sweet voice at a distance carolling the following words,

O Where has Arthur been this night
   Why did he not come home
For long the sun's fair orb of light
   hath shone in heavens dome
Beneath the greenwood tree he's slept
   his tester was the sky

O'er him the midnight stars have wept
  bright dewdrops from on high
And when the first faint streak of day
  did in the east appear
His eyes touched by the morning's ray
  shone out with lustre clear
He rose and from his dark brown hair
  He shook the glit'ring gems
Which nature's hand had scattered there
  as on the forest stems
The flowers sent up an odour sweet
  as forth he stately stept
The stag sprang past more light and fleet
  the hare through brushwood crept –

Here the voice suddenly stopped. All the trees which bordered the path rustled and Lord Charles Wellesley bounded by with so much buoyancy, merriment and elasticity that he hardly seemed to touch the ground. His rosy face was radiant with smiles, his large bright, sparkling, blue eyes seemed the transparent palaces of cheerfulness – his parted ruby lips mantling with mirth displayed a row of teeth whiter than the finest oriental pearl. His forehead, fair as ivory, was shaded by ringlets of gold which hung in beautiful clusters over his temples and his form was the very emblem of aerial symmetry. He passed the Duke without observing him as he was hid by a tall black cypress. His Grace stepped forward and called him by his name; immediately the light, gay being arrested his swift course or rather flight as soon as he heard his father's voice and turned round.

'Good morning, my son, where are you going?' said the Duke.

'O dear, dear, father,' exclaimed he. 'I'm so glad to see you; I'm going to seek Arthur who has never been home since last evening.'

'Never been home since last evening! It is true, then, they have not deceived me,' replied his Grace and the dark sorrowful cloud, which for a moment had been dissipated by the presence of his cheerful son, shadowed his noble brow more gloomily than before. 'Charles, your brother is in danger of death,' he said solemnly.

'In danger of death!' repeated Charles and immediately all gladness forsook his face and dim tears veiled his lustrous eyes. His face turned pale as ashes and, sinking on the ground, he exclaimed as well as agonising grief would permit him.

'O Arthur must not die! Little Queens can and shall save him. I will find Mystery wherever he lives. Where is Arthur, father? Where is he? I'll die if he dies, for I cannot live without him.'

'Hush, Charles, hush,' said his Grace raising him from the earth. 'Come with me into Seringapatan's cottage. I will try to save Arthur.'

By this time Seringapatan, hearing the moans and sobs of Lord Wellesley, had come out of his house. When he saw the Duke supporting his son who was weeping incessantly he was somewhat alarmed and exclaimed

'Poor thing, he seems faintish, what's the matter my Lord? Has a pekin been hurting him? Where is the wretch? Let me scald him in boiling lead but stop I'd better fetch a drink of something, for he's rather white in the face.'

'No, no, Seringapatan take him into your house a little while, I wish to speak to you.'

'O, pray come in my lord,' replied the old veteran rearing himself proudly at the thought of a secret and flinging the door wider open. 'There's nought new to listen at people's keyholes for them as lived over the ways at London.'

When they had entered, he put two chairs by the fire wiping them with a dishcloth and spreading a piece of carpet over the hearth. He then pulled a pillow from the bed-head and placed it in one chair, saying that if Lord Charles felt weakly, he might lean on it. When they were in, he closed the door, bolted and locked it and then sat down on a three-legged stool at his master's feet.

'Seringapatan,' said his Grace. 'I believe you to be an honourable and upright man, faithful to my interests and grateful for the favours I have done you. Therefore I will now trust you with a secret of great importance. Last night I received a mysterious letter purporting to be from the spirit of my dead father. It stated that Arthur, the eldest of my children and your future Lord, having, in the course of his melancholy wanderings, been drawn by the power of a secret fascination into the abode of supernatural beings, is at this moment suffering all the torments which they can devise and that if you did not go with me to a particular place which I am acquainted with, certain death will befall him and I now require you, by your allegiance to me and mine, to obey my commands in everything.' Here the Duke stopped and Seringapatan, falling on his knees solemnly promised to follow all his orders, not only at the present time, but until he should draw his last breath. The Duke then turned to Charles and asked him if he would go also, 'I would willingly die to save Arthur's life,' replied the young Lord ardently while a beam of hope lighted his glistening eyes. His father patted his curly head and smiled on him approvingly.

In a few moments they were ready and, when Seringapatan had locked his cottage door, they set out at a quick pace on their journey. In a little while, they had emerged from the forest and after crossing several hay and cornfields together with a large belt of meadow land and orchards that surrounded the village, they entered a very wide plain on which only a few scattered sheep were visible and even these in a short time ceased to present themselves to the eye. As they went on, the towers and woods of Strathfeildsay gradually sank beneath the horizon, the high church steeple lessened and receded till it became invisible, the enclosed fields and orchards vanished in the distance and, at length, only the flat plain beneath and the arched sky above remained for their sight to rest upon.

On this plain they continued till evening when they arrived at a place where were huge rocks rising perpendicularly to an immense height; a vast cataract rolling thunderously down the precipices hollowed for itself a basin in the solid stone beneath and the waters rushing over dashed furiously onwards for some time until, at length, smoothening and widening they glided peacefully along a lovely valley which opened by degrees to the right hand. It was shaded with sycamore trees and young oaks through which the rays of the setting sun now beamed with a rich lustre on the subsiding wavelets of the river, imparting to it the beautiful appearance of liquid gold. They proceeded to mount a narrow rugged sheep-path winding up one of the rocks till they came to a kind of plateau covered with herbage above which the rocks, rising to a dizzy height, appeared wholly inaccessible.

Here the Duke suddenly stopped and commanded Seringapatan and Lord Wellesley to halt as it was not necessary for them to proceed further. This he said in a tone which both his son and servant understood; it was not angry nor hardly stern, but it had a decisive sound in it which showed that no entreaties would prevail with him to let them go on. They accordingly sat down on the grass without speaking and watched him with earnest eyes for they saw it was impossible for any mortal man unassisted by supernatural power to scale the perpendicular wall of even stone which they beheld. About five yards distant from the plateau was a projecting fragment that hung over the valley beneath. It was, however, exceedingly narrow and such a tremendous height from the ground that this, together with its distance from the little plain where they were, made it perfectly improbable that any living being should dare the horrible leap which must be made before they could reach it.

The Duke stood for a moment gazing eagerly around as if searching for some means to attain his end: at length fixing his eyes on the fragment he quickly threw off his dark mantle which till now he had kept closely wrapped about him and advancing to the border of the plateau sprang from it to the ledge in an instant as if the spirit of an izard or chamois had been suddenly granted to him. When Lord Wellesley saw his father perform his daring action, to which he was prompted and encouraged by the desire to save his eldest son, a smothered scream burst from his lips. The Duke looked round, not withstanding his perilous situation and looking on him with compassion he said, 'My dear Charles, do not fear for me; in a short time I shall return with Arthur, perfectly safe and well.' Then, turning a corner of the rock, he disappeared from their sight.

Continuing on his course which became more dangerous at every step he at length arrived at a vast cavern, the entrance of which was closed with iron doors: these rolled back as he advanced and admitted him into an immense hall of stone. He entered, the doors closed after him and he found himself alone in this strange apartment dimly lighted by a blue flame in the middle. Huge massive pillars rose to the vaulted roof: their capitals were ornamented with human skulls and crossbones, their shafts were in the form of grisly skeletons and their bases were shaped like tombstones. The hall was so long that he was unable to see the end and, as he walked to and fro, he heard the echoing of his footsteps at a distance as if the sound was reflected by vaults or cells. After a considerable time the noise of an opening door was heard – light, well-known footsteps fell on his ear and in another moment he embraced his beloved son. Almost at the same instant they found themselves on the plateau were Seringapatan and Lord Wellesley anxiously waited for them.

The meeting between the two brothers was joyful in the extreme and, after a short time spent in tears of gladness and affectionate congratulating, the whole party returned in safety to Strathfeildsay. To all the questions put to the Marquis respecting his sufferings while in that cave his invariable answer has been that they were indescribable.

CHAPTER 2

It was a bright afternoon in August 1829 when the Duke of Wellington rose from the dry wearisome occupation of composing and copying state documents (better fitted for the mind of a John Herries[34] or a P. Courtnay[35] than his lofty and energetic spirit) which employment he had constantly followed for above three months without any relaxation whatsoever. After locking his writing desk and placing all the papers in order, he determined forthwith to proceed to the Horse Guards. For, tired of the tedious dull society of gentlemen in office and creeping crawling clerks, ready and even ambitious to lick the dust beneath his feet, he longed once more to breathe the fresh, free military air of that privileged retreat of all the great field-marshals, generals, staff officers and colonels now alive. Just as he had formed his resolution, the door of his apartment opened and little King and Queens entered in their usual form. They accosted him with, 'Duke of Wellington, come to Horse Guards: we are going there and we wish you to accompany us in order that you may point out all that is worth seeing.'

'I was just about to proceed thither,' replied his Grace, 'and shall be much honoured by your society.'

In a few moments they set out and, after a quarter of an hour's walk, reached the place of their destination. The gate was closed but a soldier who stood by, immediately hastened to open it as soon as he saw his Grace approach, presenting arms and making a low bow. They entered and it was shut after them. The yard of the Horse Guards was covered with rough stones and gravel, two or three sentinels were pacing about, occasionally turning their eyes towards a lofty triangle and fixed at one end on which a poor soldier was undergoing the lash of the cat-o'-nine-tails inflicted by the merciless hand of Orderly-Man who stood with his shirt sleeves rolled up exerting every sinew in the cause of cruelty.

'What crime has that fellow been guilty of to bring on his head, or rather his back, such a bloody punishment?' exclaimed the Duke as he walked towards the instrument of torture.

'He's been making faces at Lord Hill when he told him to lick the dust of his shoes,' replied Orderly-Man halting for a moment.

'Lord Hill's a scoundrel,' replied his Grace, 'in the first place for flogging a man because he refused to commit a crime (which that which he commanded him to do would have been) and in the second place for ordering you to triangle him which none but I have a right to. Take that wretch down instantly Orderly-Man. Bring Lord Hill and set him in his place.'

For the first time in his life Orderly-Man hesitated to obey his master's mandates. Casting the whip on the ground he sighed deeply, tears came into his glittering grey eyes and marks of evident grief and disappointment appeared on his rugged countenance.

'What is the matter?' said the Duke in the utmost surprise. 'I should think the fellow was absolutely under the influence of witchcraft: why don't you fly like lightning to execute my command?'

For a few moments he was unable to reply. At length, a flood of tears came to his relief and then the following words, intermixed with sobs and moans made their way,

'Well my lord, it's baking day today and I was just beginning to make a good currant cake when Lord Hill called me off to triangle this beast and now when I've done that, I'm forced to triangle him too and my cake will be eaten by Seringapatan or some other horrid glutton in the baking-room while I shall have none at all though I bought the stuff it's made of –' here as if touched by the recital of his own misfortune he wept anew. The Duke of Wellington laughed aloud and, placing his hand on his shoulder, told him not to break his heart as he would give him something better than a piece of bread – Orderly-Man, consoled by this assurance, hastened to obey his lord and, in a few minutes, Hill, suspended from the triangle, suffered the penalty of his crime.

Little King and Queens, understanding from the previous conversation that it was baking day in the Horse Guards, expressed a wish to go into the room where the bread was prepared and made ready.

'Your majesties are perfectly at liberty to do so, if you please,' said his Grace 'provided my attendance can be dispensed with, as I never frequent the apartments where the soldiers cook their food.'

'Very well, Duke of Wellington, we can do without you,' replied the fairies angrily and immediately quitting him in an abrupt manner entered the Horse Guards and proceeded to the bake-house. It was a large room built of brick without any ceiling, so that all the great beams and rafters that formed the roof were exposed to the eye, and paved after fashion of streets and thoroughfares. A fire of a sufficient size and fierceness to roast an ox was blazing at one end. A long table ran down the centre at which two or three hundred soldiers were standing, busily employed in the manufacture of coarse loaves and cakes; at the head, on a high rustic tripod sat a very old man apparently more than six feet in height with muscles as strong and supple as those of Hercules and bones as big as a mammoth's. His grizzled grey hairs were drawn all together tied with a piece of a rope and plaited into a long *queue* behind. His nose was like an eagle's beak when, by reason of its age, the upper mandible has pierced through the under and the venerable possessor, unable either to eat or drink, lies in its inaccessible eyrie, made like a charnel house by the blanched bones of those which in its vigorous youth it has slain now – I was going on but I find that the metaphor is too diffuse already. Seringapatan's nose then (for the old man was no other) was exceedingly aquiline and his mouth a scarlet thread stretching from ear to ear and, together with his fine large dark expressive eye, betokened him of true Milesian origin. He sat on his exalted throne in an attitude of extreme dignity and imperial majesty. His head, gently inclined to one side, leaned on a hand whose colour the snow might have envied, it being of a dark tawny red. One foot lay on the far side of the table and the other on the head of a horrible wretch who had ventured to rebel against his high power but who, at length, having succumbed from a gentle intimation that tomorrow at drill time he should suffer for his impudence, was now doing penance for his black crime. When Seringapatan spoke, he invariably stretched out his right arm intuward imitating the elegant action of all the great Grecian, Roman, British and Hibernian orators.

After little King and Queens had viewed this scene for some time, they left the room and proceeded to find out the Duke of Wellington. They found him in the public apartment for the officers. It was an ample rotunda carpeted with green cloth. A large brass lustre suspended from the roof was covered with the accumulated dust of several years. A billiard table stood in the middle about which a number of officers sat playing or talking. The Duke was standing at one end of the room surrounded by Lords Roslyn, Berresford,[36] Sommerset[37] and Arthur Hill together with Generals Murray,[38] Hardinge, Londonderry,[39] Fitzroy etc.[40] Roslyn was just delivering an encomium upon his Grace in the following words, 'My Lord, when you appear a mist seems withdrawn from my eyes. You are as the clear splendour of the sun shining after rain. The dark clouds hasten at your approach to mingle with the swelling waves of the deep from whence they came and to whence they will return. A hundred flowers whose beautiful heads drooped beneath the fury of the storm and whose radiant colours waned as it beat upon them, raise in their slender stems, unfurl their emerald leaflets and hold up their golden crowns towards the first beam of light which heralds your appearance, that they may be filled with loveliness and joy for, lo, you have already glorified the last drops of the departing shower into a faint but fast brightening rainbow. As I gaze on that mighty apparition spanning the whole earth and heaven, a solemn sign that the victorious waters shall never again roar triumphantly over the world's highest mountain which clave the clouds with their summits or roll in her pleasant valleys the palaces of beauty and silence. I think, by a mysterious connection of the humble snowdrop, both the arch of the sky and the first blossom of spring are alike in their origin, though one be a child of heaven and the other of earth, for each is "rocked by the storm and cradled by the blast". Eh? My lord is not that very pretty?' said he and at that moment he certainly bore a much greater resemblance to a monkey than a man.

'Roslyn,' replied the Duke smiling sarcastically, 'you have certainly outdone yourself today, though I am afraid if a jackal or a mandrill, a pinch or a pigmy could be brought to speak it would still surpass you in giving utterance to all that is conceited and devoid of sense in the compass of Apish phraseology. But, Sir, and I am now serious, if you bother me again with such language more resembling the watery scum of a weak, whining poetaster's brains than the conversation of an officer of sense and spirit or even of a civilian whose capacities are but mediocre in every respect, I shall certainly allow you the privilege of showing off some elegant French attitudes – scrapes and bows, whether of the head or the back, will, I presume, be perfectly immaterial on a triangle formed of deserter's halberds exposed to the view and derision of the whole regiment of the guards. You will likewise, Sir, be expected to attend drill every day to officiate as caller of the muster roll, to clean your own arms and accoutrements without the aid of any menial attendant, to associate with the common shoe blacks valets and squatters of the army in order you may teach them the polite art of elocution besides improving their general manners by your elegant example and, finally, you will be cashiered for a few months to the end that you may enjoy your favourite solitude which will perhaps enable you to produce more masterly specimens of rhyming than you have hitherto favoured us with.'

Here his Grace stopped. All the generals around stood staring contemptuously at Roslyn and, when he happened to come near any of them, they shrank from his touch as if he was infectious, not deigning to speak to him for a moment. Seeing their strange conduct and hearing the words of his master, the poor wretch burst into a flood of tears, sobbed aloud and then, as if unable to contain himself, he ran out of the room as fast as he was able and a few minutes after he was heard at a distance singing the following verses,

To the forest to the wilderness
Ah let me hasten now
Wher'ere I go I still shall see
My master's lowering brow

The woods black shade won't hide my grief
No influence now I have
But th' stream will give more quick relief
I'll seek a watery grave

Unto the shore I'll swiftly fly
I'll plunge into the sea
The foam bells will ascend on high
When drowning sets me free

Drown all the ills which life doth give
O mis'ry in me dwells
When no longer shall I live
The tide of sorrow swells

Suspended from an elm tree tall
I'll end my mournful life
My soul more bitter is than gall
My heart is full of strife

I'll cut my neck with some sharp blade
I'll swallow poison dire
No now my resolution's made
I'll set myself on fire!

Just then a loud noise was heard in an adjoining apartment and Gamekeeper came rushing into the room exclaiming that Lord Roslyn had thrown himself into the fire but that he had been pulled out before he was hurt.

'Take him,' replied the Duke of Wellington, 'to the lowest dungeon, keep him there and feed him on nothing but bread and water for a month.' His Grace then quitted the room and little King and Queens followed him.

'Where are you going?' said they.

'To Arthur's apartment,' he replied 'Will your majesties honour me by your company?'

'Yes,' they answered shortly and in a few minutes, after mounting a flight of stone steps, they arrived at the end of a long gallery terminated by a door which, when opened, discovered a small antechamber, where was an arched entrance veiled by a curtain of thick green baize. The Duke undrew the curtain and a most elegant, but rather small saloon, presented itself. The floor was spread with a rich Persian carpet and low sofas surrounded the room covered with green satin elegantly embroidered in needle work. A dome tastefully painted in the arabesque style formed the roof, several stands of beautiful white marble supported alabaster vases of the finest and most fragrant flowers. On the Parian mantelpiece stood a number of images classically designed and well-executed in Japan china and on a hearth-slab of costly Pabruza marble were ranged magnificent porphyry, lapis lazuli and agate vessels filled with the most exquisite perfumes the East can supply. All the windows were shaded with orange and myrtle trees which grew in large pots of Seville china. At one of these were seated the Marquis of Douro and Lord Wellesley. The former was habited in the uniform of his regiment, imperial blue and gold. The latter in white silk lightly bordered with green and a purple mantle fastened on one shoulder by an ornament of sapphire and emerald.

As soon as his Grace entered, they both started up joyfully, welcoming him to their peaceful retreat from the noisy and turbulent rotunda. In a few minutes, he sat down and then after a short silence he observed, 'What a luxurious place this is Arthur, quite unfitted, I assure you my son, to prepare a man for those hardships which everyone has to encounter during some part of his life.'

'O father!' exclaimed Lord Charles, 'Arthur will always make hardships if he has not them ready at hand. Ever since he has been here (that is three hours), I have not observed a single smile on his countenance and, after tiring myself to no purpose with trying to make him speak, I was forced to open the window and amuse myself by talking to every person who passed in the court below. At last that resource failed me for no living creature showed its head and therefore shutting the sash

I sat down again, remained silent for half an hour and then, finding that hypochondriasm was fast approaching upon me, I got up smelt at every flower and perfume in the apartment, danced, shook the orange branches, sung merry songs, stamped, raged, wept, mimicked Arthur, screamed, smiled, became hysterical fainted and, at last, finding all my efforts fruitless to provoke him to utter the smallest monosyllable, I flung myself exhausted on a seat and remained staring franticly at Arthur till you entered, when, to my inexpressible joy, I saw him rise and open his lips to welcome you.'

The Duke of Wellington remained for about an hour at the Horse Guards and then returned to Downing Street where he found a bundle of official documents awaiting his arrival. These he immediately sat down to decipher and at this employment I shall, for the present, leave him.

Volume 4

CHAPTER 1

One fine autumnal evening, the Duke of Wellington was on his way from London to Strathfeildsay. He had just passed through the village and had entered a narrow bridle path leading to the park gate. Here he dismounted from his horse and, leading old Blanco-White by the reins, proceeded at a leisurely pace onwards. It was, as I have said, a fine evening in autumn: the air was warm and breezeless, the sky covered with high, light clouds except where here and there a few pale soft blue streaks appeared on the hazy horizon. The sun had just set, the snails were crawling forth from the hedge-side to enjoy that refreshing dampness which immediately precedes dusk at this period of the year. Scarcely a leaf fell from the oaks and hawthorns bordering the path, for the dark hue of their foliage had hardly begun to mellow with the waning season. The only sounds audible were the noise of an occasional lady-clock[41] humming by and the trickle of a rill as it flowed invisibly down an ancient cart rut (now unused), hid by dock leaves, wild vetch grass and other hedge plants with which the road was completely overgrown. A hill rising on one hand concealed from view the hall with its extensive parks, pleasure grounds, gardens, woods etc situated in a broad and delightful valley sloping far down on the other side.

As the Duke walked quietly forward, he suddenly heard a murmuring sound like the voices of several people conversing in an undertone, a little in advance of him. He stopped and listened but was unable to understand what they said. At a few paces further, on a turn in the path, brought in sight the figures of three old women seated on a green bank, under a holly, knitting with the utmost rapidity and keeping their tongues in constant motion all the while. Stretched in a lounging posture beside them lay little King languidly gathering the violets and cuckoo-meat which grew around. At the Duke's approach, he started up as likewise did the old women. They curtsied and he bowed much after the fashion of a dip-tail on a stone. He then, after a sharp peal of laughter from his companions, addressed the Duke thus,

'Well, Duke of Wellington, here are three friends of mine whom I wish to introduce to you. They lived for some time as washerwomen in the family of the late Sir Robert Peel Bart who respected them so much that in his will he remembered them each for twenty guineas. After his death, however, the present Bart turned them away together with several other antiquated but faithful servants of his deceased parent, to make room for the modern trash of fopish varlets that now constitute every gentleman's establishment. Thus they are now cast on the wide world without shelter or home and if you would consent to take them into your service it would be conferring a great obligation on me as well as them.'

'I am not much accustomed to engage servants,' replied his Grace, 'but you may take them to my housekeeper and if their characters will bear the old lady's scrutiny I have no objection.'

'Very well, that's right, Duke of Wellington,' replied little King, much pleased.

The Duke then remounted his horse and proceeded at a smart trot onward wishing to escape from the company of his new acquaintance. They however stuck close to him and continued by his side talking and laughing and trying to draw him into conversation incessantly. In a short time they turned the hill and, going rapidly down a long inclined lane, entered the vast wood which forms a boundary to one side of Strathfeildsay Park – after threading the puzzling mazes of the labyrinth which leads to Seringapatan's, Orderly-Man's, Jack of all Trades' and Gamekeeper's cottages they stop at the door of Seringapatan's and the Duke stooping his head to avoid the huge thick branches waving around, lifted the latchet. Seringapatan instantly sprang out and, bowing low, without waiting for his master's orders flung open the park gate. His Grace then bent aside and whispered something in the old man's ear, commanding him to detain little King and his comrades until he reached the hall. Seringapatan bowed again lower than before and the Duke, tickling Blanco's flanks, galloped swiftly off.

'If you please, will you step into my kitchen a minute and rest you?' said Seringapatan.

They thanked him and without further ceremony walked in. It was a small apartment, neatly white-washed. An oaken dresser furnished with the brightest pewter and delftware covered one end; above it was suspended a highly polished musket and sword. Several ancient books were carefully piled on a black oak kist. Two substantial armchairs stood at each end of a hot, blazing fire and opposite the window seat, a number of stout three-legged stools were ranged in a row. The floor and hearth were as clean and white as scouring could make them. Mrs Left Seringapatan sat mending her husband's stockings by a round deal table. She was clad in a dark green stuff gown with snow-white cap and apron and looked as sedate as if she had been sixty instead of twenty-five.

When little King and the old women entered she rose and begged them to be seated: they complied. After chatting awhile, she got up again and went out but in a short time returned with a plateful of rich currant cake and a bottle of perry. These dainties she invited her guests to partake of which they did, of course, and then prepared to depart. Seringapatan, knowing that by this time his Master had arrived at his seat, opened the door and permitted them to go. They pursued their way up the park without stopping, for night was fast coming on and the moon, pouring her light on the long groves and alleys which, in dark obscure lines, stretched far over the undulating prospect, was climbing the mild autumnal heavens amid freckled downy clouds and dimly visible stars.

It happened that Lord Charles Wellesley had that day been taking one of his wild rambles over his father's domains and he was now returning homewards. At a distance, he saw the three old women with their conductor. Being fond of company he made haste to overtake them but as he approached his volatile mind changed and he determined to walk close behind and remain a concealed listener to their conversation, promising himself much amusement from the scheme. In this, however, he was deceived for voluble as they had been while in Seringapatan's cottage they now became perfectly silent.

In about a quarter of an hour, they reached the deep rapid stream which runs through the grounds. Its banks are shaded by willows and larches and the long rays of moonlight, trembling through the high boughs, fell with sweet serenity on the turbulent waves producing a soothing contrast to their impetuous and dark ridges following each other in quick succession down the waters. A grassy mole extending to the opposite bank formed a kind of natural bridge and over this Lord Charles supposed they would go, so he halted a while to observe them. They, however, to his astonishment glided noiselessly to the midst of the river and there, turning three times round amidst the shivered fragments of brilliant light in which the moon was reflected, were swallowed up in a whirlpool of raging surges and foam. He stood a moment, powerless with horror, then springing over the mound dashed through the trees on the other side and, gaining the open path, beheld little King and the three old women walking whole and sound a few yards before him. More surprised than before, he viewed them in silence for an instant and then concluded that they were other fairies whom little King had brought with him to this earth. He strove to satisfy himself with this conjecture but, notwithstanding his endeavours, he still felt an uneasy, vague and by no means pleasant sensation when he looked at their little sharp faces and heard the shrill disagreeable tones of their voices (for they were now chatting away as merrily as before) for which he was unable to account.

At length they arrived at the mansion. Little King knocked at the great gate the folding doors rolled back and a blaze of red light burst forth, illuminating the grand flight of broad sculptured steps and the dark avenue for, a great distance off, a huge fire was burning in the wide hall's chimney and every branch of the brass lustre bore a flame. The servants were gathered together at supper: Gamekeeper sat at the head of the table, Jack of all Trades officiated as waiter and Orderly-Man as vice-president. Peels of laughter rose every instant to the lofty roof and the oaken rafters trembled. Little King and his companions entered. The doors were shut again and Lord Charles was left to the darkness and solitude of night which formed a wide difference to the revels he had just caught a glimpse of. After a moment's thought, he cleared the steps with a bound and, springing along the path, came to a door in the wall which he opened with a key he took from his pocket and then entered a small green plain, delightfully planted with many beautiful shrubs and trees and watered by a fountain in the midst. This he presently crossed and, ascending a high flight of balustraded marble steps, reached a terrace that led to an arched glass door, he opened this also and a small elegantly furnished room became apparent which was his own and his brother's private apartment.

Arthur was sitting by the fire with his head resting on his hand lost in deep abstraction. The moment Lord Wellesley entered he started up exclaiming, 'Ah, Charles, I have been listening and wishing for you a long time and now I am rejoiced at your arrival – come sit down and let us have our usual pleasant *converzazione* before retiring to rest.' Charles met his brother's welcome with equal cordiality and, flinging himself on the warm Persian rug began to relate his adventures of that day, in which employment I must for the present leave him and return to little King and the three old women.

After supper was over, he requested leave to speak with the housekeeper and was informed by one of the maids that she had withdrawn for the night and they dared not now disturb her but that tomorrow he might procure an interview for himself and friends. This answer by no means pleased the dames who were beginning in a loud shrill cadence to express their dissatisfaction, when Old Man Cockney coming in they, together with the servants, were driven off to bed.

The next morning they rose with the sun and were only prevented from breaking in upon Mrs Daura Dovelike's rest by a chambermaid who met them at the door and warned them of the consequence of their intrusion – namely, instant dismissal without an audience.[42] It was with difficulty they were persuaded to wait till nine o'clock so great was their anxiety to have the affair of engagement settled. At that time Mrs Daura sent word that she was ready to receive them. On proceeding to her apartment they found her seated at breakfast in an armchair with her feet on a cushioned footstool. Her stiff figure was invested in an old-fashioned, bustling, black silk gown with cap and ruff starched to the consistence of buck-ram. As kind fortune would have it, she happened this morning to be in good temper so, after bidding them sit down and asking a few questions, she agreed to take them before her lady the Duchess of Wellington.

When they had passed through a long corridor gallery and antechamber, they came to her private sitting room. It was ornamented after a most splendid but nevertheless simple and unostentatious style. The Duchess was engaged at her usual charitable employment of working for the poor. She was attired in a rich robe of dark crimson velvet almost entirely unadorned except one bright diamond which fastened the belt. The redundant tresses of her fine brown hair were confined in a silken net over which gracefully waved a single white ostrich feather. Her face and figure were extremely beautiful and her large hazel eyes beamed with expression. But the principal charm about her was the gentleness and sweetness ever visible in her countenance. It seemed, and it was, impossible for her to storm and frown or even be angry for if anything wrong was committed by her servants or dependants she only looked grieved and sad and not dark or lowering.

When they entered, the Duke was also in the room conversing with his lady and the housekeeper on seeing him curtsied respectfully and was going away when he called her back and, quitting the apartment, left them to transact business without being under the embarrassment of his awe-inspiring-minister-general-and-clerk confusing presence. After a short conversation it was settled that the three old dames should act for one month on trial as washerwomen and laundry maids and that if, during the prescribed time, they behaved well they should then be taken into permanent service at wages of ten guineas per annum each. When this was fixed, they left her ladyship's equally delighted with the mild condescension of her manner, the enchanting benignity of her smiles and the unexpected success of their application.

The next day, they commenced the performance of the duties of their office which they continued for some weeks to execute with equal punctuality, diligence and sobriety but not without many quarrels among themselves, often ending in ferocious fights where tooth, nail, feet and hands were employed with equal fury. In these fracas little King (who always continued with them) was observed to be exceedingly active, inciting them by every means in his power to maul and mangle each other in the most horrible way. This circumstance, however, was not much wondered at as his constant disposition to all kinds of mischief was well known and he was considered by every member of the house of Strathfeildsay not excepting the Duke himself more as an evil brownie than a legitimate fairy.

Lord Charles had not revealed to anyone the strange incident, of which he was witness that happened on the first night of their arrival. His curiosity, of which he naturally possessed a considerable share, strengthened. He watched them narrowly but nothing occurred further to warrant the suspicion of their being supernatural creatures. One afternoon he went alone to that part of the river's banks whence he saw them walking on the waves, after wandering some time among the trees gathering wild roses, bluebells and other field flowers, he lay down on the green turf and fixed his eyes on the blue sky peering at intervals through the thick masses of overhanging foliage. The sounds that saluted his ear were all of a lulling, soothing character only the soft murmuring of the water flowing, the distant cooing of turtle doves from the groves or the whispering of wind in the trees. By degrees his eyes closed, a pleasing sensation of secluded rest glided through him and he was gradually passing away into a profound balmy slumber when, suddenly, an articulate voice came up on the breeze which said, 'Meet us at midnight in the corridor.' He started up and listened. The sound had died off and no trace or tone of it remained in the wild woodland music breathing around.

'I am bewitched,' he exclaimed aloud, 'those beings have certainly cast a spell over me but I will keep the assignation notwithstanding for I can do so without anyone being acquainted with it as Arthur is at London.'

He then rose and walked home. During the remainder of the day, a most unusual expression of thought appeared in his countenance and at night he retired early to his chamber. He sat pensively alone reading by a table till every noise ceased and not a voice or footstep was heard to break the dead hush reigning throughout the whole house. Then the dull, heavy toll of the great hall clock fell on his ear, twelve times the hammer resounded. He got up and extinguished his taper and quitted the room by a secret outlet opening to the corridor. His eyes glanced with an involuntary shudder down the long vista, all was veiled in impenetrable darkness. At length a bright light appeared moving among the pillars. He advanced onwards, it receded slowly from him but he still followed. After a while, he saw it ascending a stair which wound up the great round tower. There he bent his course till he gained a huge door where the light vanished and left him alone. The door, with a harsh jawing din, opened and a vast lofty chamber became visible, faintly illumined by long glimmering rows of torches which cast on all sides a bloody and terrific light. It had no roof but the sky above seemed as if a star-lit and cloudy dome. A huge black canopy in the midst swayed to and fro in the wind that rushed through the open top and underneath were set three coffins each of which held a shrouded corpse. Lord Charles advanced towards them and, turning aside the winding sheets, perceived that they were the three old washer-women. He trembled with dread and, at that instant, a loud laugh rang in his ears. He looked up and beheld little King and Queens standing beside him, one of them gave him a hearty slap on the shoulder saying, 'Charley, don't be frightened they were only our enchantments.'

He opened his eyes at this salute, stared around wondered and became bewildered. For, lo, he was lying in the pale moonlight on the rivers bank and no living creature near. He immediately ran with all haste to the house and, when he had arrived there, repeated his tale with eagerness to his father, mother and brother whom he found together in the private parlour. They laughed at it of course but on inquiry it was found that the old women had been absent from Strathfeildsay since the morning. Investigation was set on foot but no clue by which they could be traced was discovered. One countryman said that he had observed them about noon on the moor with little King, but that he had occasion to turn away his eyes for an instant and when he looked again he saw little King and Queens standing in the same place but not the smallest mark of them. This was all that could, after the strictest search, be gathered and they have never been seen or heard of from that time to this.

CHAPTER 2

It was a sweet July evening when the Marquis of Douro and Lord Charles Wellesley lay stretched on the verge of a lofty precipice, silently beholding the prospect around. Majestic forest trees waving above their heads formed, with woven intermingled boughs, a sylvan roof to the natural carpet of grass and flowers spread beneath. Far down, hundreds of green oaks and sycamores clothed the rocky and almost perpendicular shelving abyss in the dark summer verdure with which their branches were now arrayed, and from the profound depth below arose the voice of a concealed torrent hid by the gathering obscurity of dusk which was there heightened because of the gulf into which the sides of the precipice sloped that lay beyond the reach of the uncertain light lingering on the horizon after sunset. No sound save that dissipated the twilight sensation of stillness with which every passing breath of wind was charged until the Marquis, taking a guitar that lay by his side, swept its chords till every string vibrated in unison and then played an old, mournful air which, sweeping over the broad landscape, was answered from a great distance by the same tune.

'There, listen to Marian's reply,' exclaimed Lord Charles.

Arthur listened attentively but the music and its echoes in a little while died softly away. They both remained silent for some time again. Their eyes were fixed on the east where a pale light spreading over the sky began to herald the moon's advent, at length, like a silver shield, she heaved slowly up among stars and clouds and sat like empress of the night on a throne of blue hills which bounded the orient expanse of scenery.

'It is surely impossible for that orb of light to be a world like ours,' said Arthur as the splendour of its beams shone around him.

'Not at all my dear brother,' replied Lord Charles laughing, 'if you like I'll tell you a tale concerning it while we sit idly here.'

'Do, Charles, you know I always enjoy your stories particularly when I'm melancholy as I happen to be just now. Begin, love, I am ready.'

'Well I will directly but first where's my ape Tringia?[43] Tringia! Oh here he comes now, Tringia, sit down under that branch of underwood. There are some nuts and blackberries to amuse yourself with and you must be more quiet than a dove while I divert Arthur's attention from the inhabitant of that pretty house which you may see yonder, Tringia, surrounded by a garden and plantation and lo! what do I see stooping amid the flowery parterres of that garden? An object clothed all in white! It cannot be, yes it is Marion Hume![44] And now that I look better, through this small opera glass, she is watering the very rose tree that Arthur gave her from the green house and planted there with his own hands, kind youth that he was. Yes and there is her harp standing by the bower from which a few minutes ago she played that enchanting air.'

'Charles, are you going to tell me this story or not?' said Arthur, apparently wishing to draw off his attention.

'Yes, I am brother,' replied Lord Wellesley and he began as follows.

'Once upon a time there lived in Georgia, upon the banks of silver Aragua which washes the feet of the mighty Elborus, an old man named Mirza Abduliemah. He abode all alone in a solitary hut far from the habitations of men, the nearest hamlet being twelve miles distant. His occupation was that of a woodcutter an easy business for one who lived in the heart of Georgia's forests and he likewise gathered and sold the fruit of chestnut trees. Accustomed from his youth to the vast solitudes of Caucasus' giant mountains he needed not the society of human beings but loved rather to walk in the vales of young vines and lindens which smile round the borders of Aragua, to gaze at the wondrous ravines rent in the stupendous sides of icy Kasibeck or to view in mute astonishment the awful form of good Gara towering aloft and raising its snow-crowned head afar into the deep azure of his native skies.

One evening as he returned homewards, weighed down under the burden of sticks which he had gathered in a wood three miles distant from his hut, he sat him down in a little green glen between two rocks. The sky overhead was bright, cloudless and beautiful. The horizon round about was clear as liquid amber and the light which streamed from it was of the purest golden hue enriching the summits of the coniform hills with a faint glow of orange that divested the snow of that cold deadly aspect which would ill have harmonised with the transparency of warmth that tinted every other object. The aged Mirza felt himself touched with the beauteous prospect and, kneeling, he turned towards Mecca said his sunset prayers to Mahomet and then thanked the one Almighty God for his goodness in creating such a profusion of fair and lovely scenes merely for ungrateful man's pleasure and recreation.

When he had finished, he rose, resumed his bundle of faggots and casting a last look at the glorious horizon, he prepared to quit the glen, but what was his surprise on beholding a black, even line drawn around the pellucid heavens like a zone. It rose slowly up coiled itself in rings and unfurled, with a noise like the concentrated winds of heaven, two dark dragon pinions which shadowed the west as if the obscurity of thunder clouds hung over it. For a few moments it wavered between the vault of heaven and the globe of earth, then gradually descended. Mirza shook like one palsy stricken, but how was his fear heightened when he felt himself drawn powerless towards it. He prayed, he shrieked, he called on the name of Mahomet in vain, still like iron before the magnet he continued his charmed course upward. Swifter than light he fled to the sky on, on, for days and nights till the moon grew larger than the earth to his eyes. At length overwhelmed with dread he fell into a long swoon and, when his orbs of vision were released from the bondage by which they were held fast closed and sealed, he was in a land the like of which no man ever before saw. Nothing was to be seen but black mountains, higher than the highest on earth, vomiting forth floods of fire and clouds of smoke – nothing to be heard but the roaring of internal flames. The ground quaked constantly under him and was continually rending in every direction and from the ravines fresh streams of red, burning liquid burst boiling forth and overwhelmed everything near.

"I must die, I cannot live," he exclaimed aloud while the cold sweat of terror fell in large drops from his writhing visage. "O! Mahomet, O! Allah, save thy servant! What horrid crime has he committed thus to die the death of an infidel?"

"Squilish squilli keriwes Nevilah," exclaimed a sharp shrill voice above him. He looked up and beheld a creature standing on the point of a rock surrounded by several others of a similar form. But how shall I describe its shape? To what shall I liken it? It was seven feet in height, stood on legs that resembled branches of trees, its eyes were two holes in a square block that formed its head. Its mouth was invisible except by a pucker in the rugged skin when shut, but when open it was an oblong hole displaying three rows of brown teeth as sharp and slender as pins. Its arms were so long that, from the elbows downward, they rested on the ground. It, with the others, cleared the rock at one leap and alighted near Mirza. They seized and bound him with long scarves that hung on their heads and afterwards remained for about half an hour examining him closely and showing every sign of extreme astonishment. At the end of that time, Mirza heard a great hissing bubbling noise. He looked up and beheld a vast volume of lava rolling impetuously towards him, they saw it likewise and catching him up in their arms fled with incredible swiftness in an opposite direction, it however followed and would presently have overtaken them if a steep rock had not come to their relief. In a moment they sprang from it to one which stood opposite and the lava, when it reached the brink, was precipitated, with a noise like the tremendous crash and rattle of approximate thunder, down the declivity where in a short time it assumed the appearance of a black mass undistinguishable from the dense gloom of the ravine where it lay.

When this was over they hastened on without halting till day began to wane. At that time they reached a narrow vale irrigated by a branch from a neighbouring river and planted by several high trees of a kind unknown on earth. One which far outdid the rest in loftiness and beauty, spreading its huge branches for a vast extent around, bore among thickly clustered leaves and blossoms hundreds of strange appearances like the nests of great birds. To this the beings, who still carried Mirza with them, directed their steps and quickly ascending the trunk and boughs took possession of the topmost of these nests and snugly ensconced themselves there behind an entrenchment of rich purple and golden streaked fruit growing luxuriantly on one side of their circular habitation. When they had plucked and eaten themselves they offered some to Mirza. He tasted it at first warily but finding that it proved gratefully refreshing to his palate, though the flavour was different from any he had ever before known, he ate freely and without restraint. When the repast was concluded they all sat perfectly silent having their eyes fixed on a certain point of the sky which was azure like that which canopies our world. Mirza looked in that direction also and began mentally to repeat his evening prayers.

Scarcely had he commenced when a light appeared over the hills. It slowly rose and, when all was revealed, Mirza saw his earth in the form of a great luminary five times larger than the moon seems to us. He bowed his head and thanked God in silent ejaculations. Then all his companions turned away, as the earth rose and coiling themselves round in the nest presently gave Mirza notice by loud snores that sleep had closed their eyelids. Somnous[45] also soon asserted his empire over him and in the oblivion of a deep sleep he buried his woes for the space of one lunar night which is, I believe, Arthur, much about the length of a terrene.

How long he continued with these strange creatures I cannot say for I never heard but his deliverance from them happened thus. One day when they were all gone down from the tree in search of fruits and had left him alone, he knelt and earnestly implored for liberty at the hands of Mahomet who it seems heard and accepted his petitions, for before he had finished, he was startled by the sound of wings and ere he could look up an immense feathered and pinioned animal of marvellous form and dimensions had him safely secured in its great brazen claws. He calmly resigned himself to his fate without one shriek or struggle, imagining that these judgements coming so thick and fast upon him one at another's back were for some dreadful crime that his fathers had committed. The moon eagle, for it was nothing else, quivered for a while over the valley and then rose perpendicularly to an immense altitude. Mirza feared that it was mounting to the sun and, in that case, he knew that the eternal torment of fire was certain to be his portion. Again his fervid, though inward, prayers were sent up to the great Prophet, the eagle waved its wing, loosened the strong grasp of its talons and Mirza found himself whirling at rather an uncomfortable rate downward.

Of the particulars of his descent I am ignorant as, long before he arrived at a landing place, sense had fled his skull. When, however, it returned he was reposing on the ground and two gigantic forms were bending over him. Their countenances and figures were majestically beautiful, shaped like those of human beings. Instead of ears they had long flaps of flesh hanging gracefully down on their shoulders. Their hair was soft and glossy as unspun silk, in colour a pale blue, arranged in artful wreaths and curls upon their heads. From their foreheads projected a long taper horn, white and polished as the finest ivory, and a string of gold beads was wound spirally about it. Their attire was a long robe of white down, bound at the waist with a richly embroidered belt and falling thence in the softest and most elegant folds. Their arms and ankles were adorned with bracelets of gold and their feet with sandals of down ornamented by silver bands and fastened with jewels. From their necks also hung several strings of precious stones and gold or silver. They were gazing at Mirza in smiling astonishment turning him over and examining him with the utmost gentleness and care and conversing to each other meantime in a strange but harmonious language.

After some time spent thus, they rose and, wrapping him in the leaf of a huge plant that grew near, they conveyed him towards a great plain where was a very large and magnificent tent surrounded by several meaner ones. This they entered, passing through formidable ranks of armed giants between thirty and forty feet in height, all of whom showed them the greatest respect. In the midst of the tent sat one who appeared to be the chief, in a thoughtful attitude, his right hand supported his monstrous head and his left a dagger. They advanced and unfolding the leaf placed poor little unfortunate Mirza before him. He gave an exclamation, apparently of delight, snatched him up and rising hastily quitted the tent making a sign that none should follow.

For about the space of an hour he walked or rather strode on over hills plains and rivers till there appeared a valley full of tents that encompassed a palace-like edifice constructed of a species of variegated marble not in the best architectural taste but from its enormous bulk inspiring an idea of sublimity and grandeur. This was the metropolis of the country where Mirza was and that building was its king's residence. The giant directed his course thither.

It would be needless for me to give an account of the odd ceremonies that took place on his introduction to the king which, besides being tedious, would make my tale even dryer than it now is, Arthur. But when they were over, he showed Mirza with a joyful countenance to his majesty who leapt from his throne in a transport and on resuming his seat poured forth an energetic speech expressive of his joy. Then Mirza was consigned to a golden box enriched with gems where he lay a miserable captive till next day. At that time, he was taken out and food was offered to him. Being extremely hungry he ate though with great loathing and disgust as he knew what animal it was the flesh of and the taste was coarse and disagreeable.

Just when he had concluded his repast he heard a tremendous sound of shouting instruments and music etc. He was then placed in his box and hurried off. After many hours of marching he was again let out and found himself in the midst of a vast army of giants who were ranged at a respectful distance from an altar where he stood in the hands of a venerable old priest clothed in wide, flowing garments with a snow-white beard hanging lower than his girdle and long grey hair dishevelled in the wind. A great fire burnt on the altar and, as he sprinkled perfumes thereon and anointed Mirza with fragrant oils and essences, he uttered these words, "Here is the sacrifice which thou didst demand, O Mountain! Here are our warriors assembled to do thee homage. Accept our offering and spare us!" By these words Mirza knew his doom for, though spoken in a strange tongue, they were supernaturally understood by him. He trembled and quaked with horror as the idea of being burnt alive flashed through his mind but no shriek or supplication burst from his whitened lips and, after some inward strife, he resigned himself to his inevitable fate hoping that the joys of Paradise would be his subsequent reward. The priest now poured the last libation over his devoted head and bathed him in the blood of a newly slain beast and more fuel was added to the fire whose flames were already ascending with intense fierceness and heat. Mirza was on the point of being dropped headlong in when a cry of horror broke from those around. The priest withheld his arm and looked up. A huge black mountain appeared in the sky wavering over their heads and slowly descending on them. Suddenly, a flood of fire burst from the summit and a terrible voice was heard to say, "Have ye, O wretches, provided the offering?" "We have," they all exclaimed in an agony of dread. With a dull rumbling sound it went up again while they watched it in breathless silence while every trace vanished from the heavens.

The priest then turned to Mirza and said, "Creature, whoever thou may'st be, thou art doomed to die for our safety. We, for a length of time, have been tormented by that vision which thou sawst. It threatened to destroy us if a being like thee was not procured to appease it by death; at length some good spirit has placed thee in our power. Thou wert found by the daughters of our chief warrior, asleep and defenceless in a field. They brought thee to their father and by him thou wast delivered to our king. Hitherto thou hast behaved with becoming resignation. Let not thy heart fail thee in the hour of death –"

With these words Mirza was committed to the flames and the tortures he endured were hard and indescribable, for, as the fire seized his feet and legs, he felt all the sinews crack the calcined bones started through his blackened cindery flesh; by degrees his extremities crumbled to ashes and he fell prostrate amid their ruins. A short time now sufficed to extinguish his insupportable agony. The rising smoke presently suffocated him and he died amid shouts and cries of gladness from his sacrificers.

The remnant of my parched tale is clad in a veil of mystery. This same Mirza who suffered the extreme rigour of the law among those giants was, I know not how long subsequent to that event, wakened from his sleep of death by a shake on the shoulder which brought life again into him. He looked about and discovered that he was standing upright against the door cheek of his hut with a bundle of faggots lying before him. His surprise and joy I will not attempt to depict but on examining his hands and feet he found that they were all marked with long seams and scars of burning. This staggered him a little but after some consideration he concluded that it was all the machinations of those evil spirits who haunt the Caucasian range. For my part, I do not agree with him but think that these circumstances I have related really occurred. Mirza never knew whether the giants were inhabitants of the sun, moon, stars or earth. I believe the latter.'

'Well, my sons, what witch- or wizardcraft is going on between you that you have need to do it under the midnight (or there-abouts) moon and sky? Come home my young scape-graces,' exclaimed a voice close behind them. They started to their feet and saw their father standing near.

'I'll come directly,' replied Lord Wellesley. 'Tringia, Tringia, where are you?'

Tringia sprang from under his branch of brushwood and, in a short time, was seated in softer and warmer quarters with Trill,[46] Philomel[47] and Pol on the rug of the private parlour before a warm blazing fire...

That is Emily's, Branwell's, Anne's and my land
And now I bid a kind and glad goodbye
To those who o'er my book cast an indulgent eye.

NOTES

1. Taby was the Brontës' servant from 1824 until her death a few weeks before Charlotte's own.

2. The Duke of Wellington, Lord Arthur Wellesley (1769–1852), was the main hero of Charlotte's childhood writings.

3. Lord William Cavendish Bentinck (1774–1839) was a soldier and statesman who became Governor-General of India.

4. Rebels who re-occur throughout the juvenilia.

5. C.N. may refer to Colonel Naughty, the identity of S. and T.O.D. is unknown.

6. Fictional troublemaker

7. Character based on John Gibson Lockhart (1794–1854), who was one of the main contributors to *Blackwood's Magazine.*

8. Personifications of Branwell, Charlotte, Emily and Anne

9. Arthur, Marquis of Douro, based on Arthur Richard Wellesley (1807–84), Wellington's real-life eldest son, who would replace his father as the hero of Charlotte's juvenilia.

10. Lord Charles Albert Florian Wellesley, based on Charles Wellesley (1808–58) the second son of the Duke of Wellington, was Charlotte's favourite pseudonym throughout her juvenilia.

11. Sir Alexander Hume is a surgeon, based on Dr John Robert Hume (1782–1857) who was surgeon to the Duke of Wellington.

12. Sir Astley Cooper is a surgeon, based on Sir Astley Poston Cooper (1768–1841) surgeon to the King in 1828.

13. Sir Henry Halford is a surgeon, based on real surgeon to George III and his three succeeding monarchs.

14. Family based on that of Edward Baines (1774–1848) the proprietor and editor of the *Leeds Mercury*, an influential Whig newspaper. He had three sons, Matthew (a lawyer), Edward and Thomas (both newspaper editors). Charlotte disliked Edward, in particular, for his opposition to Tory policies.

15. Strathfeildsaye, Duke of Wellington's Hampshire estate, usually spelled Strathfieldsaye.

16. Fictitious veteran of the Peninsula War, now employed by the Duke of Wellington.

17. From the French, *Pékin*, the word used by Napoleon's soldiers to describe a civilian.

18. Character possibly based on Leopold I, son of the Duke of Saxe-Coburg-Saalfeld (1750–1806), who later became the first king of Belgium.

19. Character possibly based on Rowland, first Viscount Hill (1772–1842), who served under Wellington and later became Commander-in-chief of the British army

20. The Marquis of A. may denote Arthur Parry, Marquis of Ardah, who was to become a significant character in the Angrian tales; Lords C.A.W. and G.P. are unidentifiable.

21. An 'Extra-Ordinary Issue' was published by the *Leeds Intelligencer* in 1829, outlining the terms upon which Roman Catholics were to be allowed to vote and hold office, a subject about which the Brontë family felt very strongly.

22. Fictitious veteran of the Peninsula War, now employed by the Duke of Wellington.

23. Character based on Auguste Jules Armand Marie, Prince de Polignac (1780–1847), who was an ultra-royalist French statesman and Prime Minister under Charles X.

24. Character possibly based on King George IV (1762–1830), then Prince Regent.

25. Character possibly based on Queen Victoria (1819–1901), then Princess Victoria prior to her succeeding two uncles to the throne in 1837.

26. Fictitious veteran of the Peninsula War, now employed by the Duke of Wellington.

27. Fictitious veteran of the Peninsula War, now employed by the Duke of Wellington. Named after Seringapatam, the stronghold of Tipu Sultan and scene of a decisive battle in 1799, also known by his first name Left.

28. Fictitious veteran of the Peninsula War, now employed by the Duke of Wellington.

29. Character based on John Scott, 1st Earl of Eldon (1751–1838), a Tory politician who served twice as Lord Chancellor.

30. Character based on Henry Hardinge, 1st Viscount Hardinge (1785–1856), who was a Field Marshal and Governor-General of India.

31. Poet and butt of the jokes in Wellington's entourage

32. Close friend of the Marquis of Douro, based on Robert Stewart, Marquis of Londonderry, Viscount Castlereagh (1769–1822) who was an Irish and British statesman.

33. Sir Robert Peel (1788–1850), was a Tory politician, twice elected as Prime Minister and who oversaw the formation of the Conservative Party.

34. John Charles Herries (1788–1855), was a politician and Cabinet member under Wellington.

35. Character based on Thomas Peregrine Courtenay (1782–1841), who was a politician and writer.

36. Character based on William Carr Beresford, Viscount Beresford (1768–1854), who was a British general, later Master of the Ordinance under Wellington.

37. Character probably based on Fitzroy James Henry Somerset, first Baron Raglan (1788–1855), who was aide-de-camp and military secretary to the Duke of Wellington.

38. Sir George Murray (1772–1846), career soldier and politician, Secretary of State for War and the Colonies in Wellington's cabinet

39. Charles William Stuart, 3rd Marquis of Londonderry (1778–1854), was a soldier, politician and nobleman.

40. Robert Fitzroy (1805–65), was captain of HMS *Beagle* and later Governor of New Zealand.

41. Ladybird

42. Wellington's fictitious housekeeper at Strathfeildsay, possibly based on the Brontës' Aunt Branwell.

43. Lord Charles Wellesley's pet monkey

44. Daughter of Sir Alexander Hume, heroine of Charlotte's writing, she became the Marquis of Douro's wife, only to die of a broken heart due to his infidelities.

45. Roman personification of sleep

46. Lord Charles Wellesley's pet kitten

47. Lord Charles Wellesley's pet nightingale

NOTE ON THE TEXT

This edition contains a reworked transcription of the four volumes of *Tales of the Islanders*, which Charlotte Brontë wrote out over the period of a year (1829–30) in small hand-made books. While a complete set of stories in themselves, the island tales form part of Charlotte Brontë's extensive juvenilia and introduce some of the characters that reappear in her later stories, which are set for the most in the imagined kingdoms of Angria and Verdopolis. As in Charlotte's other tales, the four Brontë children all appear here in various guises, and in particular as little King and little Queens.

BIOGRAPHICAL NOTE

Charlotte Brontë was born in Thornton, Yorkshire, in 1816. In 1820 her father was appointed curate at Haworth Parsonage where Charlotte was to spend most of her life. Following the death of her mother in 1821 and of her two eldest sisters in 1825, she and her two surviving sisters, Emily and Anne, and brother, Branwell, were brought up by their father and a devoutly religious aunt.

Theirs was an unhappy childhood, in particular the period the sisters spent at a school for daughters of the clergy. Charlotte abhorred the harsh regime, blaming it for the deaths of her two sisters, and she went on to fictionalise her experiences there in *Jane Eyre* (1847). Having been removed from the school, the three sisters, together with Branwell, found solace in storytelling. Inspired by a set of toy soldiers, they created the imaginary kingdoms of Angria and Gondal which form the settings for much of their juvenilia. From 1831 to 1832 Charlotte was educated at Roe Head school where she later returned as a teacher.

In 1842 Charlotte travelled to Brussels with Emily. They returned home briefly following the death of their aunt, but, soon after, Charlotte was back in Brussels, this time as a teacher. At great expense the three sisters published a volume of poetry – *Poems by Currer, Ellis and Acton Bell* (1846) – but this proved unsuccessful, selling only two copies. By the time of its publication, each of the sisters had completed a novel: Emily's *Wuthering Heights* and Anne's *Agnes Grey* were both published in 1847, but Charlotte's novel, *The Professor*, remained unpublished in her lifetime. Undeterred, Charlotte embarked on *Jane Eyre* which was also published in 1847 and hailed by Thackeray as 'the masterwork of a great genius'.

She followed this up with *Shirley* (1849) and *Villette* (1853), and continued to be published under the pseudonym Currer Bell although her identity was, by now, well known.

Branwell, in many ways the least successful of the four siblings, died in 1848. His death deeply distressed the sisters, and both Emily and Anne died within the following year. Charlotte married her father's curate in 1854, but she died in the early stages of pregnancy in March 1855.

SELECTED TITLES FROM HESPERUS PRESS

Author	Title	Foreword writer
Pietro Aretino	The School of Whoredom	Paul Bailey
Pietro Aretino	The Secret Life of Nuns	
Jane Austen	Lesley Castle	Zoë Heller
Jane Austen	Love and Friendship	Fay Weldon
Honoré de Balzac	Colonel Chabert	A.N. Wilson
Charles Baudelaire	On Wine and Hashish	Margaret Drabble
Giovanni Boccaccio	Life of Dante	A.N. Wilson
Charlotte Brontë	The Spell	
Emily Brontë	Poems of Solitude	Helen Dunmore
Mikhail Bulgakov	Fatal Eggs	Doris Lessing
Mikhail Bulgakov	The Heart of a Dog	A.S. Byatt
Giacomo Casanova	The Duel	Tim Parks
Miguel de Cervantes	The Dialogue of the Dogs	Ben Okri
Geoffrey Chaucer	The Parliament of Birds	
Anton Chekhov	The Story of a Nobody	Louis de Bernières
Anton Chekhov	Three Years	William Fiennes
Wilkie Collins	The Frozen Deep	
Joseph Conrad	Heart of Darkness	A.N. Wilson
Joseph Conrad	The Return	Colm Tóibín
Gabriele D'Annunzio	The Book of the Virgins	Tim Parks
Dante Alighieri	The Divine Comedy: Inferno	
Dante Alighieri	New Life	Louis de Bernières
Daniel Defoe	The King of Pirates	Peter Ackroyd
Marquis de Sade	Incest	Janet Street-Porter
Charles Dickens	The Haunted House	Peter Ackroyd
Charles Dickens	A House to Let	
Fyodor Dostoevsky	The Double	Jeremy Dyson
Fyodor Dostoevsky	Poor People	Charlotte Hobson
Alexandre Dumas	One Thousand and One Ghosts	

George Eliot	*Amos Barton*	Matthew Sweet
Henry Fielding	*Jonathan Wild the Great*	Peter Ackroyd
F. Scott Fitzgerald	*The Popular Girl*	Helen Dunmore
Gustave Flaubert	*Memoirs of a Madman*	Germaine Greer
Ugo Foscolo	*Last Letters of Jacopo Ortis*	Valerio Massimo Manfredi
Elizabeth Gaskell	*Lois the Witch*	Jenny Uglow
Théophile Gautier	*The Jinx*	Gilbert Adair
André Gide	*Theseus*	
Johann Wolfgang von Goethe	*The Man of Fifty*	A.S. Byatt
Nikolai Gogol	*The Squabble*	Patrick McCabe
E.T.A. Hoffmann	*Mademoiselle de Scudéri*	Gilbert Adair
Victor Hugo	*The Last Day of a Condemned Man*	Libby Purves
Joris-Karl Huysmans	*With the Flow*	Simon Callow
Henry James	*In the Cage*	Libby Purves
Franz Kafka	*Metamorphosis*	Martin Jarvis
Franz Kafka	*The Trial*	Zadie Smith
John Keats	*Fugitive Poems*	Andrew Motion
Heinrich von Kleist	*The Marquise of O–*	Andrew Miller
Mikhail Lermontov	*A Hero of Our Time*	Doris Lessing
Nikolai Leskov	*Lady Macbeth of Mtsensk*	Gilbert Adair
Carlo Levi	*Words are Stones*	Anita Desai
Xavier de Maistre	*A Journey Around my Room*	Alain de Botton
André Malraux	*The Way of the Kings*	Rachel Seiffert
Katherine Mansfield	*Prelude*	William Boyd
Edgar Lee Masters	*Spoon River Anthology*	Shena Mackay
Guy de Maupassant	*Butterball*	Germaine Greer
Prosper Mérimée	*Carmen*	Philip Pullman
Sir Thomas More	*The History of King Richard III*	Sister Wendy Beckett
Sándor Petőfi	*John the Valiant*	George Szirtes

Francis Petrarch	*My Secret Book*	Germaine Greer
Luigi Pirandello	*Loveless Love*	
Edgar Allan Poe	*Eureka*	Sir Patrick Moore
Alexander Pope	*The Rape of the Lock and A Key to the Lock*	Peter Ackroyd
Antoine-François Prévost	*Manon Lescaut*	Germaine Greer
Marcel Proust	*Pleasures and Days*	A.N. Wilson
Alexander Pushkin	*Dubrovsky*	Patrick Neate
Alexander Pushkin	*Ruslan and Lyudmila*	Colm Tóibín
François Rabelais	*Pantagruel*	Paul Bailey
François Rabelais	*Gargantua*	Paul Bailey
Christina Rossetti	*Commonplace*	Andrew Motion
George Sand	*The Devil's Pool*	Victoria Glendinning
Jean-Paul Sartre	*The Wall*	Justin Cartwright
Friedrich von Schiller	*The Ghost-seer*	Martin Jarvis
Mary Shelley	*Transformation*	
Percy Bysshe Shelley	*Zastrozzi*	Germaine Greer
Stendhal	*Memoirs of an Egotist*	Doris Lessing
Robert Louis Stevenson	*Dr Jekyll and Mr Hyde*	Helen Dunmore
Theodor Storm	*The Lake of the Bees*	Alan Sillitoe
Leo Tolstoy	*The Death of Ivan Ilych*	
Leo Tolstoy	*Hadji Murat*	Colm Tóibín
Ivan Turgenev	*Faust*	Simon Callow
Mark Twain	*The Diary of Adam and Eve*	John Updike
Mark Twain	*Tom Sawyer, Detective*	
Oscar Wilde	*The Portrait of Mr W.H.*	Peter Ackroyd
Virginia Woolf	*Carlyle's House and Other Sketches*	Doris Lessing
Virginia Woolf	*Monday or Tuesday*	Scarlett Thomas
Emile Zola	*For a Night of Love*	A.N. Wilson